GRANDMA'S
ATTIC NOVELS

*Wedding Bells
Ahead*

ARLETA RICHARDSON

Cook Communications

You'll enjoy all the books in Arleta Richardson's Grandma's Attic Collection

Jamie produced a sodden packet of papers and placed it on my desk. "It had some kind of box around it, but that fell apart. The papers got kind of wet and runny."

"Where did you find them, Jamie?" I asked.

"They were under the corner of the well house that the tree tipped over," he replied.

He disappeared through the door, and I spread the soaked papers out on the desk to dry. A date at the top of the first page caught my attention: September 9, 1861.

Curiously I scanned the paper and then, forgetting that this was none of my business, I went back and read it again. . . .

Cook Communications Ministries,
Colorado Springs, Colorado 80918
Cook Communications, Paris, Ontario
Kingsway Communications, Eastbourne, England

WEDDING BELLS AHEAD
© 1987 by Arleta Richardson

Previously titled NINETEEN AND WEDDING BELLS
AHEAD

Cover illustration by Steve Armes, PGS Advertising
Cover design by Manoutch Kazemzadeh, PGS Advertising

First printing, 1987
Printed in the United States of America
04 03 02 01 00   5 4 3 2 1

Library of Congress Cataloging-in-Publication Data

Richardson, Arleta
        Nineteen and wedding bells ahead.
                (Grandma's attic series.)
                Summary: The time before Mabel's wedding is
busy as she teaches school and prepares for her new life as a
preacher's wife.
                [1. Christian life—Fiction] I. Title. II. Series.
PZ7.R3942Ni   1987   [Fic]   87-461
ISBN: 0-78143-292-8

To Alice Kenworthy Bedell,
my "Sarah Jane," who
has always known the meaning
of the word friend

Contents

Ma Has
A Surprise

I'VE NEVER KNOWN IT TO RAIN ON MY BIRTH-
day," I said, leaning back against the big
tree at the corner of the lane and gazing
up at the canopy of leaves over our heads.

"This won't last long, Mabel," Sarah Jane
assured me. "When the drops are this big,
there are never many of them."

"Do you suppose this is an indication of
things to come?"

"By all means. You've never been nineteen
years old before. The possibilities for disaster
are unlimited."

"Sarah Jane, be serious. I don't mean that
I think everything will go wrong, but you'll
have to admit that it will be a different year
than we've ever had before."

Sarah Jane nodded. Apparently she decided not to tease me into a different frame of
mind, for she lapsed into silence. She had
been a part of my life longer than any other
person outside my family, and her boast that
she knew me better than I knew myself was
not an idle one. I could recall many times

when my world might have collapsed had Sarah Jane Clark not been there to support it.

"Are you still trying to decide what you should do about a school next year?" she said finally.

"I was waiting for you to make that decision," I grinned. "You've never failed me yet."

"I *could* come up with something slightly less ridiculous than I've heard you suggest so far," she replied.

"I'm not being ridiculous," I protested. "You know I can't live with the Williams family now that Len and I are engaged. The only practical thing to do is to find a position in another district."

"You sound as though North Branch had only one house in it," Sarah Jane snorted. "There has to be a better solution than leaving town. I'd set up a cot in the back of the schoolroom before I'd give up a place I loved."

I had to laugh at the thought, though the situation seemed serious to me. My first year of teaching in the little country school had been a success, in spite of several near disasters and one very hostile parent. I felt good about the way the children had learned and the wonderful friends I had made. And best of all, of course, was the fact that Leonard Williams had asked me to marry him.

"You're lucky that Len's father is the board president," Sarah Jane was saying. "If it had been anyone else, you might not have been offered the school again. After all, you did break your contract by falling in love."

"That's true," I nodded. "But I still can't go back there to live. Len said he would get a room in town, but I couldn't let him do that."

"It certainly is tiresome, not being able to do what is most convenient because people's tongues will wag."

"Especially when I know they're going to wag anyway. I can just hear Augusta Harris if I stayed in the same house with Len, even though his folks were there."

Sarah Jane's eyes lit up. "That's it! Augusta!"

"Don't even suggest it!" I said hastily. "You know I couldn't live with Augusta for a whole year."

"Be reasonable, Mabel. She's all alone, she has room, and—"

"And she bites," I finished. "I'm on the receiving end of her caustic remarks often enough without setting up housekeeping with her."

"It was only a thought," Sarah Jane said

with a shrug. "I just can't see you having to leave North Branch because of a place to live. Staying with Augusta seems like a practical solution."

"Thanks, Sarah Jane. Even the cot in the back of the schoolroom sounds appealing by contrast."

The rain had stopped. As we ambled back toward the house, I thought fondly of my first year of teaching at the little school in North Branch. As far as I had heard, there were no new children in the community. With the exception of Abe Lawton, who had left before school ended this year, my class would be the same if I returned.

"Len says I don't have to be afraid of Cy Lawton this next year, anyway," I told Sarah Jane. "He knows better than to call attention to himself in that county, since his wife reported him for beating Abe."

"That's one point in your favor," Sarah Jane replied.

"But I'm not so sure about his daughter Elizabeth," I confided. "I don't think she'll hover in the background just because Len asked me to marry him. She's a determined individual."

"So are you, Mabel. And Len chose you, not Elizabeth."

"I'll be surprised if she considers that the

final word. She'll think of some way to complicate my life."

Sarah Jane laughed. "I'm glad to hear you making plans to go back, even though you're convinced that nothing but trial and tribulation await you."

"Not really," I replied. "There are a lot of happy things about that little school. I love the children, and I love teaching. Unfortunately, I'm also fond of a comfortable place to live."

"It'll work out," Sarah Jane promised. "There's a place in North Branch with your name on it."

I eyed her suspiciously. "Why aren't you campaigning harder for Augusta Harris?" I demanded. "I know you think that's where I should go."

"It's your birthday; I'm being good to you." She changed the subject. "It was sure nice to see our old friends from high school today, wasn't it?"

"Yes," I agreed. "It's a shame they all had to hurry back. And I'll admit I was a little sorry not to have Russ Bradley here. The six of us had good times in school, didn't we?"

"The best. But that chapter is closed."

I nodded. "I made the right choice. I'm not regretting it."

The rain started again, and we ran the last

few steps to the porch. I opened the screen door just in time to see Ma totter from the stove to the table and sit down heavily.

"Ma!" I exclaimed. "What's the matter?"

Her face was pale, but she smiled. "I just felt a little dizzy, that's all. I'm fine."

I was alarmed. Ma had never been sick, except for one bout with pneumonia when I was little.

"Don't you think you'd better lie down? Shall I send Pa for the doctor?"

"Certainly not, Mabel," Ma said briskly. "I'm perfectly all right. I felt this way before you were born."

I looked at her blankly. "That was nineteen years ago, Ma."

Sarah Jane laughed. "I think your ma is trying to tell you that you're going to have a new brother or sister."

It was my turn to drop into a chair, gazing at Ma in bewilderment. "You're having a baby?"

She nodded happily. "We're so pleased. The house has been too quiet the last year."

"But, Ma, you're already a grandmother. Aren't you a little . . ."

"Old?" she prompted. "Of course not. I was only twenty-one when you were born. And I didn't have this convenient home to live in." She looked around her kitchen fondly. "The wind and snow sifted into that little log cabin all winter. Reuben and Roy were only four and two, and I had my hands full, I can tell you. This baby will be a joy to care for."

"When will it be, Mrs. O'Dell?" Sarah Jane asked. "Does Ma know about it?"

"Oh, yes, your mother knows," Ma laughed. "It will be the end of November or the beginning of December. But I haven't time to sit here doing nothing. I've got to get this kitchen cleaned up."

I jumped up. "Oh, no, Ma, I'll clean up the kitchen. You sit still. Better yet, go and lie down."

"Whatever for?" Ma sputtered. "I'm not sick. You two run along and do whatever you were going to do. This is your birthday, and I want you to have a nice one."

"I have had, Ma. The dinner with all our friends was wonderful. I wouldn't have let you work that hard if I'd known," I added reproachfully.

"That's precisely why you didn't know," Ma replied. "I didn't want you fussing over me all day."

Pa came into the kitchen and hung up his hat.

"I see the news is out," he remarked. "What do you think of our second family?"

"I haven't really taken it in yet, Pa," I

answered. "But if you and Ma are happy about it, then I will be. I won't be home to enjoy a new baby, though. Why didn't you do this ten years ago? *That's* when I wanted a sister."

"And have you and Sarah Jane wear the poor thing out before its first birthday?" Ma said. "No, I think the Lord directed this correctly.

"What makes you think you're getting a sister?" Pa asked. "I could use a boy to help around the place."

"It's a girl, Pa. With violet-colored eyes and brown curls."

"Your folks might be able to face another daughter, now that you've grown up to be a fairly sensible young woman," Sarah Jane commented. "Of course, she may not have someone like me to keep her on the straight and narrow . . ."

"That will definitely put her in the disadvantaged class," I said. "But maybe Ma and Pa will have an easier time of it."

It was hard for me to imagine a new baby in my home. I wasn't even sure that I liked the idea. But as the summer went on, my feelings changed.

"I can hardly wait until we have a little one in the house again," Ma said. "It makes me feel about ten years younger."

As I sewed for the coming school year, Ma worked on little garments. It was impossible not to be touched by her enthusiasm.

"I don't think I've ever seen Ma look happier," I told Sarah Jane. "It's like a whole new life beginning for her."

"I'm sure it will be. And isn't she fortunate to have gotten you out of the way before she started it?"

When I failed to react, Sarah Jane shook my arm. "Mabel, are you there? What's the matter with you, anyway?"

"I don't know," I sighed. "I guess there are too many things to think about right now. What if Ma *is* too old to have this baby? And what if I don't have a new school *or* a place to live?"

"Has the Lord ever failed to take care of you in the past?" Sarah Jane demanded. "Why should you doubt Him now?" Then her voice softened. "You have had a lot of new situations to face the last few months. Come on; you need a change of scenery. Let's go to town and look around—maybe even splurge on some ice cream!"

"You're right," I agreed. "I'm turning into a real gloom peddler. An afternoon in town will make a new person of me."

We picked up the mail on the way to the

ice-cream parlor, and Sarah Jane spotted the letter from Len before I did.

"Open it, Mabel. You haven't seen him since Sunday." She waited expectantly.

"Don't you have any mail of your own to read?" I inquired.

"Nothing that can't wait. What does he say?"

"Sarah Jane, do you intend to move in with us when we get married?"

"Of course not!" she replied indignantly. "Why would you ask a thing like that?"

"I just wondered," I replied. "You *are* waiting for me to read this letter to you, aren't you?"

"Certainly." She complacently spooned ice cream into her mouth as I tore open the envelope.

Dear Mabel, I read aloud,

It seems like three weeks instead of just three days since I've seen you. I'm glad there is only a month until school starts again.

I have some good news for you: Augusta Harris has offered to let you stay with her this year. I think that's an excellent solution to our problem. You'll be near school, and she'll take good care of you—

I dropped the letter on the table and

gave a deep groan.

"A most intelligent young man," Sarah Jane said. "If you recall, I said exactly the same thing."

"And if *you* recall, I said I was not going to spend a year with Augusta," I retorted. "You and Leonard can both forget it. It's not even a remote possibility. . . ."

2

A New Family

I MOVED IN WITH AUGUSTA THE WEEK BEFORE school began.

"I declare," she said as Len carried my trunk into the spare room. "Looks like at least three of you coming. Do you really get around to using that much stuff?"

Len grinned and went back to the buggy for the boxes of books and school materials.

"I didn't bring anything I don't need, Augusta," I said. "I'll try to keep it out of your way."

"At least Augusta is an excellent cook," Len offered as we rode back to the Williams farm. "You'll be well fed."

" 'Man does not live by bread alone,' " I replied glumly. "It's going to be a long year."

Mrs. Williams attempted to console me as we sat around the familiar table in her kitchen. "Augusta has a good heart. She isn't always the soul of tact, but she means well. You and Alice got along all right when you lived there last year, didn't you?"

I nodded. She was referring to the time that her niece Alice and I had stayed with Augusta while Leonard had scarlet fever.

"That was weeks, not months," I said. "But I shouldn't complain. It was gracious of her to take me in, considering how much she values her privacy. I'll do my best to keep peace with her."

"I'll try not to be a bother, Augusta," I said when I returned to her home that evening. "I'll help you all I can."

"No need," she replied. "I'm not too old to take care of things, even if you young folks do think so."

"Oh, I didn't mean that I thought you were old," I assured her. "I just meant that you would have extra work."

"Can't deny that," she said, "but I was never one to shirk my duty as I see it. Won't be like living alone, but I reckon I can get used to it." She gazed at me reflectively. "You may not be the most sensible young one I've ever seen, but you're not as empty-headed as some I could mention, either."

I took that as a compliment and went to my room to unpack, determined not to let Augusta's remarks upset me.

"After all, I have Len and his folks, and I'll have you on weekends," I had told Sarah

Jane. "And we won't have to have anyone come for us this year. Len wants me to take Regal when we go home."

"True love," Sarah Jane had commented. "Any man who will share his horse is really smitten."

I agreed. I was blessed to have Leonard Williams. The time until we could be married couldn't go too fast for me.

School opened on Monday, and I was pleased to see fifteen children lined up at the steps when I went out to ring the bell, Len had accompanied me to school and raised the flag, just as he had done a year before.

"No matter how much things change, they stay the same, don't they?" I said.

"That sounds good if you don't stop to think about it too long," Len said with a grin. "But I know what you mean. It doesn't seem like a year since I carried your books for the first time. Now, the Lord willing, I'll be carrying them for the rest of your life."

"You think I'll be teaching school as long as I live?" I laughed. "Wait until Augusta hears that. She says I'm just putting in time until we get married." Len waved good-bye and left as I stood aside to let my students enter the schoolroom. I looked at them and smiled—it was good to be "home."

For the first time in anyone's memory, there was no beginner class.

"Good," Teddy Sawyer asserted, when I mentioned the fact. "Those babies are a real pain. Someone always has to look out for them."

"You were a beginner once," Josie Abbot said accusingly.

"And not very long ago, either," his sister Hannah reminded him. "And you're not any less a pain because you're in the third grade."

"This is hardly the way to start a new year, is it?" I said. "I'm sorry I brought it up. Suppose you tell me what you did this summer that was fun."

As the children mentioned swimming in the pond, the Sunday school picnic, and trips to town, my mind drifted back to the long, hot summers of my childhood when Sarah Jane and I found so many things to do. I returned to the classroom with a jolt to hear Teddy shouting angrily at Edward Alexander.

"You never! You never! I know where you went this summer, and you never went to no circus!"

"Theodore!" I said sharply. "Come here, please."

Sullenly, Teddy got out of his seat and

stood before my desk.

"Whatever is the matter with you today? Did you get out on the wrong side of the bed?"

Teddy looked surprised. "There's only one side to get out of. The other one's next to the wall."

"That's just a saying, Teddy. It means that you got up feeling cross. Why were you shouting at Edward?"

" 'Cause he said he went to the circus, and he never did."

I looked at Edward.

"Well, I *wished* I could," he mumbled.

"I'm sure you did," I replied. "Many of us didn't get very far from home this summer. But we are going to have a good time in school. Carrie and Prudence, will you hand out the books?"

The rest of the day passed smoothly, and by dismissal time we were settled into a routine of sorts. Elsie Mathews stopped by the desk after school.

"I'm glad you're back, Miss O'Dell," she said shyly.

"Thank you, Elsie," I replied. "So am I. I missed all of you this summer. How is your mother?"

"Fine. She wants you to come and have supper with us one evening." She paused.

"Shall I wait and walk home with you?"

"You don't need to wait," I told her. "Don't you walk home with some of the other girls?"

She shook her head and turned toward the door. "I don't mind being alone."

"All right," I said. "I'm almost ready to leave. I'd like to walk with you."

Augusta had tea and fresh cookies ready when I came in. "Don't know how you stay so little with all the food you put away," she commented. " 'Taint as if you were out working in the field all day, either. Schoolteachers have a pretty soft job."

I opened my mouth to disagree, then decided against it. Instead I took another cookie.

"Augusta, hasn't Elsie Mathews ever had any close friends?"

"Don't know that she has," Augusta replied. "She's always been a quiet one. She and Prudence Edwards play together at picnics and such, but they live in opposite directions. Why do you ask?"

"She just seems rather lonely. I don't mind having her walk home with me, but I wish she had friends her own age."

School had been in session about two weeks when Elsie arrived one morning looking more animated than I'd ever seen her.

"Miss O'Dell, guess what! The place next

to ours has been sold, and Pa heard the new owners have children! Wouldn't it be wonderful if there was a girl?"

"It would indeed!" I said. "When do they arrive?"

"This week. They're coming from Ohio."

"We'll look forward to having them," I told her. "We have plenty of space for more children in our room."

"I hope they're boys," Joel Gage put in. "What we need is more boys."

"Nobody *ever* needed more boys," Hannah retorted. "Girls are much nicer to have around."

"Which would you rather have, Miss O'Dell?" Prudence asked.

"Do you think I'd take sides in an argument like that?" I laughed. "I like boys and girls equally well. Whichever they are, we are going to welcome them."

"Have you heard about the new family coming?" I asked Len that evening.

He nodded. "I can't understand why they would move out here instead of buying a place in town. He's a lawyer, not a farmer."

"That does seem odd," Mrs. Williams said. "Maybe he's tired of the law and wants to farm for a while."

Len shook his head. "He's already leased

his acreage to Curt Mathews to work. If he's planning to support his family on the cases he'll get in this town, he may be in for a surprise."

The Graysons arrived at the end of the week, and Elsie gave me all the details on Sunday after church.

"They have two children," she reported. "There's a girl my age and a boy in the fourth grade. They weren't unpacked to come to church today, but I'll bring Serena and Daniel to school with me tomorrow."

Serena, I thought. *That's a nice, calm name.* Would it be too much to hope that my new seventh grader would live up to it?

"I think I'll take some bread to the new folks," Augusta announced on Monday morning. "She's likely not had much time to bake yet."

"That will be nice, Augusta," I said. "I'm sure they'll appreciate it." *And you'll find out all about them,* I added to myself. There would be no secrets about the Graysons with Augusta on the trail.

The girls were on the school grounds when I arrived. Serena reached her hand out to me.

"Good morning, Miss O'Dell," she said. "I'm Serena Grayson, and this is my brother Daniel." She grabbed a small boy who was

27

racing past us. "Say 'good morning,' Daniel."

" 'Morning!" he shouted. I looked down at a mischievous, grinning face. I liked Daniel immediately.

"Good morning, Daniel," I said. "We're glad to have you here." He nodded and continued on his way, and I turned to his sister.

"And we're glad to have you, too, Serena. It will be nice for Elsie to have someone her age living nearby. I hope you'll be happy here."

"Thank you," Serena replied. "I've never attended a one-room school, but I'm sure it will be interesting."

The others were arriving, and Daniel lost no time in joining the boys in a game of stickball. We could hear him over the hubbub of the yard.

"Daniel is not a quiet child," Serena informed me. "Mama keeps reminding him to lower his voice to a roar, but it doesn't do any good. You get accustomed to it after a while."

It was time for the bell, and we lined up at the steps, the children eyeing the newcomers curiously. Serena took her place beside Elsie and Prudence, and Daniel joined Hannah Sawyer in the fourth row. We opened the day as usual with the salute to the flag, Bible reading, and prayer. A different student read the Scripture each morning, and I asked Serena if she would like to read for us.

"Certainly," she replied. "I'll be glad to." She came to the front of the room and took the Bible I had opened to the day's verses. As I listened to her read in a clear voice, I had the feeling that this eleven-year-old was a little too cool and placid. It was hard to tell what she was thinking about her first morning at North Branch School.

Our science lesson that afternoon described various kinds of clouds, and we went outside to identify the ones in the sky.

"Isn't God good to give us such beautiful weather?" I remarked.

"We don't know if there is a God," Daniel bellowed.

Mouths dropped open, and all eyes turned toward the new boy.

"You don't know?" Teddy gasped. "*Everybody* knows about God!"

"Not us," Daniel replied. "Do we, Serena?"

Serena looked distressed, but she answered calmly. "Papa isn't really sure that God exists. But he said that if you prayed in school, we must be polite and bow our heads." She seemed to sense my thoughts, for she said to me, "It's all right to read the Bible. Papa says it is excellent literature, and a well-educated person needs to be acquainted with it."

As the day went on, Serena and Daniel worked well with the others. The children seemed to have forgotten the unexpected announcement, but I knew that by nightfall there wouldn't be a home in the valley that hadn't heard that the Graysons didn't believe in God. The ones the children didn't reach, Augusta would.

3
Augusta Refuses An Offer

AUGUSTA WAS BUSTLING ABOUT THE kitchen when I got home, and I waited for her version of the day's news. She said nothing about the Graysons, however, and I settled down to work on my lessons for the next day. When supper was ready, I cleared my books away and set the table for us. Augusta talked about the weather, the washing, the eggs, and the dress material she had found.

Finally I ventured to ask. "Did you take bread to the Graysons this morning?"

"Of course, I did. Said I would, didn't I?"

No other comment was forthcoming. This wasn't like Augusta, and I probed further.

"Did you invite them to church?"

"Certainly. They'll be there Sunday."

"The children said their parents question whether there is a God," I blurted, forgetting my silent disapproval of Augusta's love for spreading news.

"Bosh," Augusta replied. "No one is born believing there is no God. That's something they had to learn. And if they learned it, they can unlearn it."

"But we're Christians, Augusta," I said. "Shouldn't we try to convince them that they're wrong?"

"Hitting them over the head with the Bible isn't going to prove that we have the truth," Augusta declared. "We have to *live* like Christians."

"Augusta is absolutely right," I said to Len when we discussed it later. "But I don't understand why the Graysons would consent to come to church if they truly are agnostics."

"I think they want to belong to the community," Len replied. "If it's the custom of people here to attend church, they'll attend church. They don't intend to be convinced of the error of their ways. We'll just pray that there will be enough of God in our lives to cause them to question their beliefs."

"I met Mr. Grayson in town today," Mr. Williams told us. "Seems like a pleasant young man. Says he's interested in buying land here and developing homesteads."

"There hasn't been a new family in the North Branch area since the Lawtons settled here more than twenty years ago," Mrs. Williams commented. "I don't know whom he intends to sell those homesteads to."

"He could sell one to me if I had the money to pay for it," Len said wistfully. "It's a good thing Mabel knew I didn't have anything but a hole in my pocket when she agreed to marry me. But we'll have a home," he declared as he hugged me. "We'll have a nice home."

"I never doubted it," I said. "Anywhere you are will be a nice home to me."

"My grandmother Gage has come to live with us," Joel informed me one morning. "She's awful old, but Ma says she knows more than all the rest of us put together."

"Old people can have a lot of wisdom," I replied. "Where has your grandmother been living?"

"With Pa's sister—but Grandma likes the country better than the city. She says they have trolley cars that will knock you right down if you don't watch them! *I'd* like to live in the city."

"Pa says North Branch is going to be a city one day," Daniel said. "He's found a good place for a lumber mill. He says he can—"

"Daniel," Serena interrupted, "hush. You talk too much."

In the weeks that followed, Serena and Elsie were inseparable. I was pleased that they got along so well together. The Gray-

33

sons continued to attend church regularly, and Len reported that Jerome Grayson had stopped by several times to talk with him.

"We discuss a variety of things," Len replied, when I asked what they talked about. "He's interested in the economy and the future of North Branch. He doesn't think we've done all we could to utilize the resources of this area."

"Do you ever mention spiritual things?"

"You mean do I preach to him?" Len laughed. "No. He knows I believe that God still has a hand in His creation and cares for individuals. Jerome admits that some unknown power rules the world, but he's convinced that man is in charge of his own fate. We don't argue about it."

I went home almost every weekend because of my concern for Ma. Len understood, though I knew he would have preferred that I stay.

"I enjoy having you here and appreciate your coming," Ma told me in late September, "but it's not necessary for you to look after me. I'm doing just fine."

"I know you are, Ma, but should you be canning tomatoes?" I asked.

"What else would we do with them?"

"I'm afraid you'll get too tired," I replied.

"If I get tired, I know where the chair is," Ma said. "Honestly, Mabel. You fuss like an old mother hen. Don't you have any problems at school to occupy your mind?"

"Not really," I replied. "Things are going rather smoothly. It's easier when you know the children and have some idea what to expect from them."

"I wouldn't become too complacent if I were you," Ma warned me. "Life has a way of taking unforeseen turns when you aren't looking."

I arrived home from school one afternoon to find Augusta staring out the window of my room. I peered over her shoulder at the backyard and the woods beyond it. "What are we looking for?" I asked.

"*We* aren't looking for anything," Augusta replied. "I'm wondering what that Mr. Grayson is looking for."

"Mr. Grayson! Is he back there?"

Augusta nodded. "Has been all afternoon."

At that moment, Jerome Grayson emerged from the woods and walked purposefully toward the house.

"Mercy! He's coming here." Augusta smoothed her apron and started for the front door. "What do you suppose he wants?"

I knew that unless the earth opened up

35

before suppertime I would hear every word that passed between them, so I spread the day's papers out on the desk and settled down to correct them. But I didn't have to wait for Augusta's report—their voices carried clearly to my room.

"Won't you sit down, Mr. Grayson?"

"Thank you. It's a lovely day, isn't it?"

"It is," Augusta replied. "But you didn't come to tell me that, did you?"

"No," he said. "As a matter of fact, I came to ask if you know who owns the wooded area behind your place."

"Of course I do. My brother owned all the land from here to the river."

"Owned?"

"He died in the War Between the States."

"Oh, I'm sorry." Mr. Grayson hesitated. "Then I suppose the property passed to his family."

"He didn't have any family but me," Augusta declared. "He never married."

"Then *you* own the land," Mr. Grayson persisted.

"I suppose I do," Augusta replied, "though I've never seen a deed to it. Now why is it that you are so interested in the place?"

"I'd like to buy it, Miss Harris. I'm prepared to offer you a good price for it."

This was obviously an unexpected thought

to Augusta, for she didn't reply for several seconds.

"My grandfather claimed this land in 1790, Mr. Grayson. He built this house. There's been no one but Harrises here since then, and there won't be as long as I'm alive."

I could tell that as far as Augusta was concerned, the conversation was closed. But Mr. Grayson was undaunted.

"But, Miss Harris, you've no one to leave it to. You could live comfortably the rest of your life on what I'm prepared to give you."

"I would not live comfortably anywhere but in my own home," Augusta snapped. "You are wasting your time, Mr. Grayson. I've no intention of selling."

"If you should change your mind, I'll be happy to talk with you again," Mr. Grayson replied amiably. "Good day, Miss Harris."

When I heard the door close firmly behind him, I ventured out to the kitchen.

"The idea!" Augusta sputtered. "Wanting to buy a person's home right out from under them! He has a place of his own out there that he doesn't even work. What could he want of another one?"

Daniel's remark about a lumber mill came to mind, but I thought it might not be the time to mention it. At any rate, Augusta had already made her decision.

Len admitted that he knew about the offer when I spoke to him.

"Jerome has an eye for the future," Len said. "He can envision a successful mill back there. Augusta's land borders the river, and there must be several thousand acres of timber that has never been touched. If she could be persuaded to sell, she'd be a wealthy woman."

"You mean you think Augusta should give up her home, too?" I asked in surprise. "Where would she go?"

"I don't think she should do anything she doesn't want to do," Len replied. "I know her roots run pretty deep. But a lumber mill would bring a lot of jobs and new people to the area."

"There must be other stands of timber," I protested. "Isn't there some government land he could get?"

Len shook his head. "Not located on the river *and* the railroad. Augusta has the ideal spot."

"Why do you suppose he didn't tell her what he wanted the land for?" I wondered. "Not that it would have made much difference, I'm afraid."

"I'm sure he'll approach Augusta again," Len said. "He's not one to give up easily. I have a feeling he'll get what he wants."

"Len, he wouldn't do anything crooked to get the property, would he? After all, he isn't a Christian."

"I've known some people who call themselves Christian that I wouldn't trust behind a lace curtain," Len replied. "But, no. I believe Jerome Grayson is an honest man. If he does get that land, it won't be by deceit."

For the time being, the matter was closed. Mr. Grayson seemed to have accepted Augusta's refusal and turned to other concerns. For her part, Augusta continued to monitor the affairs of the community as fall reluctantly slipped toward winter.

4

Toby's Discovery

OCTOBER WAS NOT THE "BRIGHT BLUE weather," the poet promised. It rained and blew and was generally unpleasant. So, at times, were the children.

"Miss O'Dell, Toby juggled my arm and ruined my writing lesson," Nancy Lawton complained.

"Jiggled," I said. "I'm sure he didn't do it on purpose."

"Yes, I did," Toby asserted. "She snitched my new slate pencil."

"You have two. You don't need two."

"Nancy," I said, "it doesn't matter how many he has. They belong to him, and you've no business helping yourself to one. Give it back, please."

If order was restored in the second grade, it did not extend to the third and fourth. I was putting a lesson on the board when Hannah Sawyer called out, "Miss O'Dell, look at Teddy!"

I turned to see what Teddy Sawyer might be doing. When I did I found two innocent brown eyes looking my way.

"Well?"

"He keeps turning around and making faces at me. He's mad 'cause I told Pa he left the sheep gate open."

"Teddy, keep your face toward the front of the room, please. Both of you finish your lessons."

I returned to the board.

"He kicked me, Miss O'Dell!" Hannah wailed.

"Teddy!"

"I never turned around! You just said to keep my face—"

"I know what I said," I interrupted. "I also know what I'm going to do if you don't settle down. I don't want to hear any more from any of you."

Quiet was restored until recess time when everyone departed for the playground in spite of the blustery weather. I put George Elliot in charge and told him not to call me unless someone was in danger of being annihilated.

It was not just the younger children who reacted to the windy weather. Carrie Lawton had been moping about school for several days. She didn't have a lot to say to any of us in the best of times, and I searched for some way to draw her out. Nothing I said elicited more than a "No, ma'am" or "Yes, ma'am." Her schoolwork was done acceptably, so I finally decided to leave her alone until she was over the sulks.

But if Carrie was silent, her sister Julie Anne was not. I heard more about the Lawton family than I wanted to know.

"Carrie doesn't like it 'cause she has to wear Elizabeth's old dresses," Julie Anne informed me. "She thinks Pa favors Elizabeth because she brings money home every week. Carrie says she won't even *come* home once she gets out to work."

It occurred to me that given the circumstances in the Lawton home, I probably wouldn't either. I hadn't seen Elizabeth since school started, and I was glad to keep it that way. I didn't know whether or not she attended church on Sunday mornings, and I didn't inquire.

Mr. Williams's birthday fell on a Saturday, and Augusta and I were invited to have dinner with the family. Len's cousin Alice and her husband were there, as well as his two sisters and their families. All together there were sixteen of us around their big table. I then realized that this was the first time I had been a part of a Williams family gathering, and I listened with interest as they reminisced about the past.

"The house looks smaller than it did when we all lived here, Ma," Lillian commented. "I used to think this kitchen was huge."

"Especially when we had to scrub it," Frances chimed in. "Len never would remember to take his boots off outside." She looked at me. "You don't know how lucky you were not to have a younger brother, Mabel. You can't imagine what a pest one can be."

"You mean a younger one causes more suffering than two older ones?" I laughed. "That hardly seems possible."

"I'm so glad Leonard has chosen a nice, quiet girl like you to marry," Lillian said. "I didn't think that oldest Lawton girl would leave him alone long enough to let him even look at anyone else. What was her name?"

"Elizabeth," Frances supplied. "She's planned on marrying him since they were five years old. I imagine she's mighty disappointed."

"Furious is more like it," Augusta sniffed. "She hasn't liked Mabel since she first set eyes on her. I can see trouble from that one."

"Let's talk about something pleasant," said Len. "Alice and John, how are you coming on your house?"

I was grateful to have the conversation

turn. Elizabeth's name didn't come up again until Len had left Augusta and me on our porch at the end of the evening.

"Mark my words," Augusta said. "Elizabeth hasn't given up on Len yet. She's a sly one, and she knows how to take advantage of Len's good nature."

Remembering some of the tricks Elizabeth had pulled the year before, I was tempted to believe Augusta—but I wouldn't admit it.

"I think she knows better than to pursue him now that we're engaged," I said. "I don't intend to waste my time worrying about Elizabeth Lawton."

"Don't say you weren't warned," Augusta said. "You'd be wise to keep an eye on that young man of yours—especially on the weekends when you're off home."

"If I don't trust Len, I have no business planning to marry him," I replied. "Besides, how am I going to watch him while I'm home?"

Augusta had no answer for that, and I went to get ready for bed.

So she is *here on the weekends,* I thought, as I lay staring into the dark. *She wouldn't dare try to get Len away from me now.* I tried to comfort myself with the thought that Augusta had a habit of expecting the worst.

Later that week I returned from school to

find Augusta seated in the rocker with her hands folded in her lap.

"Augusta, are you sick?" I asked.

"Of course not," She snapped. "I'm never sick. A waste of time."

"Oh. Well, you're usually doing something . . ."

"I *am* doing something. I'm thinking." She watched as I took off my coat and started for my room. "I had another visit from that Mr. Grayson today."

I turned around and came back. "He still wants to buy your place?"

She nodded. "He was quite insistent. He's willing to give me more than I ever knew it was worth. Makes me a mite suspicious. What do we know about him, anyway? He wouldn't be the first city slicker to try to cheat an old lady out of her living."

"You aren't an old lady, Augusta," I told her. "And I'd like to see the city slicker that could cheat you out of anything. Besides, Len is sure that Mr. Grayson is an honest man."

"Len thinks the best of everyone," Augusta replied. "I try not to let Mr. Grayon's lack of faith color my opinion, but how far can you trust a man who thinks God doesn't pay any attention to him?"

I had no answer for that. The same thought had crossed my mind, but I did have confidence in Len's good instincts.

"One thing is for sure, Augusta," I said. "You don't have to sell if you don't want to. It isn't as though Mr. Grayson could foreclose on you or anything like that."

She nodded, but I could see that she was worried. I thought perhaps if Len talked with her, it might ease her mind. But before I could mention it to him, something else came along to occupy my own.

The younger children were digging in the dirt at the corner of the schoolhouse when Toby called to me.

"Look, Miss O'Dell. See what we found."

I came to investigate, and the others gathered around us. The digging had revealed a good-sized rock beneath the frame structure of the building.

"It's got writing on it," Rosie exclaimed. "What does it say?"

We brushed the dirt away and read the inscription. "North Branch of Chippewa River School. 1792."

"That's the name of our river," Jamie said. "Is that what North Branch used to be called?"

'Has the school really been here that long?" Elsie wondered. "If it has, it's a hundred years old this year!"

Toby sat back on his heels and looked at

the building. "A hundred years! That's older than my pa!"

"It's older than your grandpa, too," George laughed. "I wonder if Grandpa knows the school is having its hundredth birthday this year."

"Let's have a party!" Prudence suggested. "Everyone in North Branch could come. Most of them probably went to school here."

"Who do you suppose is the oldest one living?" Joel said. "It might be my Grandma Gage."

"There must have been a lot of teachers here in a hundred years," Carrie said. "Some of them are still alive. We could invite them to a party."

"Recess is over," I said. "Let's go inside and talk about it. You've raised a lot of interesting questions."

"Could you find out the answers for us, Miss O'Dell?" Teddy asked.

"I could," I said, "but I think it would be better if you found them yourself. Suppose we plan a hundred-year celebration and present a history written by the upper grades?"

"Oh, yes!" Elsie exclaimed. "We could make it into a pageant, and everyone in school could have a part!"

"All right," I agreed. "We'll do it for our

Christmas program. But you'll need to start right away, and it will mean a lot of work."

"Where do we begin?" Prudence asked. "How will we ever find out all we need to know?"

"I suggest that each of you ask the oldest person in your family what he or she remembers about the school. Write down who their teachers were and the names of any schoolmates they remember. We'll bring all the information together and sort it out. What one person has forgotten, another one may remember."

"The oldest person in my family is my pa, and he never went to school here," Carrie said.

"He never went to school *nowhere*," Julie Ann chimed in.

"Anywhere," I corrected her. "He may remember the names of some of the teachers."

"We don't have anyone to ask," Serena said. "We've only been here a month."

"There are some people in the valley whose families have been here for years," I told her. "Miss Harris doesn't have children in school, but I know she could tell you a lot about the history of North Branch. Why don't you talk to her?"

Serena's face brightened. "That's a good

idea! I was afraid I'd be left out of the celebration."

"Nobody will be left out," I said. "Everyone will have an important part."

"I think Toby should have the best part," Edward declared. "He's the one who found the rock."

"He will certainly have full credit," I agreed, and Toby beamed. "Now suppose you write down the questions you want answered, so you won't forget anything when you talk with your families or neighbors."

I looked at the heads bent over their papers and slates and thought what a wonderful lesson in history this would be. Had I known what a Pandora's box would open in the next few months, I would not have been so complacent.

5

What the Storm Revealed

LEN WAS ENTHUSIASTIC WHEN I TOLD HIM about our project.

"Pa has school records for as far back as they were kept," he said. "I'm not sure how many years that is—maybe not a hundred, but close to it."

"I'm not going to tell the children that," I laughed. "I want them to find out as much as they can from their families. We can fill in any missing spots from the records."

"This should be interesting," Mrs. Williams said. "Maybe we'll find out who set fire to the school in 1834. As I recall, no one owned up to it then."

"You mean the school was burned down?" I asked.

"Twice," she said with a nod. "Burned again in 1875 when Lillian and Frances were in school. We don't know who did it that time, either. Maybe your young ones will find out."

"Don't be surprised if one of them comes to you," I told her. "They're excited about gathering their information. Serena Grayson is going to talk to Augusta."

"She's tapping the right source," Mr. Williams put in. "There's *nothing* Augusta doesn't know. That program ought to pack the schoolhouse out."

I explained to Augusta what we were doing.

"Serena wants to talk to you, because your family was one of the earliest settlers in this part of Michigan, wasn't it?"

"The first, so far as I know," Augusta replied. "Not a whole lot of people were brave enough to come in here. The Chippewa Indians were hereabouts, and my pa remembered Grandpa Harris bargaining with them."

"Were you living right here when the War Between the States started, Miss Harris?" Serena asked when she came to question Augusta. "Do you remember who was in school back then?"

"Yes, indeed," Augusta began. "Frank Gage was in the sixth grade and Ellen Gage in the seventh."

"Is that Mr. Gage, Joel's father?"

"That's right. And Frank's eldest sister kept company with my brother John. They were both out of school by the time the war started—John was nineteen."

I half listened as Augusta continued her story, thinking how interwoven the lives were in this little community. The Lawtons and the Graysons were the only older children in school whose families didn't go back several generations. What a marvelous story it would make!

I paid closer attention when I heard Augusta say, ". . . John was afraid the North might be invaded, so before he left for the war, he buried the box. Don't know what was in it, but it couldn't have been very valuable. We didn't have anything worth much except this place."

"But didn't he dig it up after the war?" Serena wanted to know.

"Didn't come back. Like as not Ma took care of it, but I don't remember."

"Thank you, Miss Harris. You've helped a lot. I guess no one knows more about North Branch than you do."

"Hmmph," Augusta replied. "Don't tell everything I know, either."

I was pleased with the information the children brought in. Surprisingly, there was little conflict in their reports.

"The school had two teachers one year when my pa was here," George Elliot told us. "The big boys ran one of them off because he used the stick on 'em too much."

"No one would run you off, would they, Miss O'Dell?" Edward asked. "You'd stand right up to them!"

He didn't seem to expect an answer, for which I was grateful. I was quite confident in my ability to manage my school without the use of physical force—but I was glad I had never been tested.

"Grandma Gage remembers clear back to 1816 when she started school here. She says there's been a Gage here ever since the school was built," Joel said.

"There's been an Elliot every year, too," Jamie contributed. "And they've all been boys—every one of 'em!"

"You mean there's never been any girls in your family?" Prudence demanded. "In a hundred years?"

"My ma's a girl!" Toby declared indignantly.

"Of course she is," I soothed him. "Prudence just means that it's unusual to have a family of boys who have no sisters. That makes your family special."

Other people remembered interesting facts about the school and community, and little by little we began to see a good picture of the earlier years. When Mr. Williams brought out the records, I had fun going back over the attendance sheets.

"Jamie was right," I remarked to Len. "There has been at least one Elliot boy in school every year. It looks like a Gage every year, too."

"Joel's the last one for a while," Mrs. Williams put in. "They lost two boys a few years back in a flu epidemic, and Marcie left North Branch when she got married five years ago. She was named for Frank's oldest sister."

"I heard about her," I said. "Isn't she the one Augusta's brother was interested in?"

"A sight more than interested, I'd say," Mrs. Williams replied. "They were to be married as soon as he came home from the war."

"How sad. Where is she now?"

"She died just months after he did. I know it was a tragedy that John Harris was killed, but Marcie wouldn't have been alive when he got home, anyway. She was consumptive."

"Augusta Harris finished school in 1843 and John in 1855. That was the last of the Harris family, too, wasn't it?"

Mrs. Williams nodded. "Too bad Augusta never married. Might have taken some of the edge off her disposition. I always thought she had her eye on Frank's uncle, but nothing came of it."

October's weather did not improve as the

month drew to a close. The wind howled around the schoolhouse, and rainstorms came unexpectedly.

"I guess Pa and I will have to bring wood in early this fall," George Elliot said to me one day as we shivered in the chill air. "We don't usually start fires until November."

I agreed. We would have a lot of sick children if they continued to sit around with wet feet in our cold room.

At home, Augusta was concerned about the strong winds.

"That old tree by the well house is doing a lot of creaking," she said. "If it goes over, I hope it has the good sense to fall toward the well instead of the house. Maybe I'd better have Hiram Elliot take it down before a good storm gets it."

I returned home from school on Thursday afternoon in the midst of a gale. Cold rain fell, and the wind seemed to come from all directions at once. Augusta held the door open for me.

"Mercy!" she said. "I thought you were going to be blown right on past the house. Don't know when I've seen a storm like this in October. Get those wet clothes off and come out by the fire."

"You're right about that old tree," I said when I came back into the kitchen. "It's

55

stopped creaking and started groaning. I'm sure it's going to fall over."

"Best you stay in this part of the house tonight," Augusta said. "If it comes this way, it will land on the roof over your room."

I was only too glad to stay in the kitchen to work that evening. The fire roared in the stove, and as I graded papers and studied for the next day, I was thankful for a warm, safe place to live. When it was time for bed, I brought my blankets and pillow out to the couch. The wind continued to shriek around the corners of the house, and I fell asleep thinking that the little ones would probably not be able to get to school in the morning.

The tree fell in the night.

"Thank the Lord," Augusta said, when she found that the roof had not caved in. She peered out into the blackness from the window of my room. "I can't see where it went. I'm just glad to know where it *didn't* go."

The morning light revealed the well house tipped crazily toward the woods, the huge roots of the tree having pushed it casually out of the way.

Augusta surveyed the mess glumly. "I'll miss that old tree. I'd rather have the shade than the firewood. But it's an ill wind that blows no good. Hiram and George can make some money chopping it, and I'll have my woodshed full for the winter."

She returned to the kitchen to get breakfast, and I began to prepare for school. Glancing out the window, I caught a glimpse of Jamie and Toby Elliot climbing over the fallen tree, talking together excitedly. Rain was still falling steadily, but the boys were unaware of anything except the giant that towered five feet off the ground, even in its horizontal position. Their father and brother would undoubtedly still be working on it when the younger boys came home from school tonight.

The wind had died down, and the sun was beginning to make a tentative appearance as I opened the schoolhouse. I was putting lessons on the board when the door burst open and Jamie Elliot raced to the front of the room.

"Did you hear the tree fall, Miss O'Dell? Aren't you glad it didn't hit the house? Do you want to see what we found?"

"Yes, yes, and yes," I replied, laughing. "Slow down, Jamie. One question at a time. Now, what did you find?"

Jamie produced a sodden packet of papers from his pocket and placed it on the desk. "It had some kind of box around it when we picked it up, but that fell apart," he exclaimed. "The papers got kind of wet and made the ink runny."

"Where did you find them, Jamie?" I asked.

"They were under the corner of the well house that the tree tipped over," he replied. "Actually, Toby found them. He wanted to take them home for Pa to see. Pa said we should have taken them right in to Miss Harris, but Toby's too little to know any better."

"You could have dropped them off there on the way to school," I suggested, not mentioning that *he* was not too little to know better.

Jamie nodded. "We stopped at the house, but Miss Harris was gone. So we brought 'em to you." He started for the door, then called back, "George won't be here today. He's working with Pa. Wish I was big enough to help on the cross-saw. I wouldn't be here either!"

He disappeared through the door, and I decided to spread the soaked papers out on the desk to dry. The ink had smeared in many places, and I hoped they would be legible enough for Augusta to make out what they were.

I didn't intend to read them, but a date at the top of the first page caught my attention: September 9, 1861. That was the year the War Between the States started, and Augusta had said that her brother had buried something. Perhaps this was it, although it certainly didn't look very valuable. Curiously I scanned the paper and then, forgetting that this was none of my business, I went back and read it again:

I, John Harris, on this 9th day of September, 1861, do will the property described in this deed to my wife, Marcie Gage Harris. In the event that I do not return, I request that Marcie Gage Harris provide a home for my mother, Julia Harris, for the remainder of her life, and for my sister, Augusta Harris, until she be married.

There was more concerning the property, but I had seen enough. I was certain that Augusta knew nothing of this, since she had said that her brother had never married.

I might as well not have been in school myself that day, for I paid scant attention to geography, math, or English. My mind whirled with uncertainty about what I must do. Should I just hand the papers to Augusta, and not let on I knew what was in them? Or should I hide them again and pretend they had never been found? The truth was, I had no desire to be a part of the scene when Augusta discovered she no longer had a legal claim to the Harris land. . . .

6
A Problem for Augusta

INSTEAD OF GOING HOME AFTER SCHOOL, I went directly to the Williamses', where I found Len in the barn.

"This is a pleasant surprise," he said happily. "I didn't expect to see you until this evening."

"It's a surprise, all right," I replied, "but I'm not sure how pleasant it's going to be."

I gave him the packet, and he sat down on a bale of hay to look at it. His face grew serious as he read.

"What should we do, Len?" I asked, after telling him how the papers had come to light. "It was a real temptation just to put them back. After all, if it hadn't been for the storm, they probably would never have been found."

Len shook his head. "I don't think we can do that," he said. "This looks like a valid deed to the property. It belonged to John Harris, and his wishes should be carried out."

"But what will Augusta do? Besides, Marcie Gage has been dead for years."

"Her family isn't," Len reminded me.

"Oh, I wish these old papers had never been found," I wailed. "They're going to cause nothing but unhappiness and trouble."

"But they have been," Len replied, "and we're responsible to see that something is done with them. Perhaps we should talk with Jerome Grayson about it."

"You keep them," I said as I rose to leave. "I don't want to take them home and run the risk of Augusta finding them. This is so unfair! Why should she have to lose her property and home when she has no one to take care of her?"

"I'm sure she'll be cared for," Len said. "The Gages wouldn't leave her homeless."

"I'm in favor of burying those horrid papers where they won't rise again until the resurrection," I muttered.

"It's about time you got here," Augusta said as I came through the door. "I've been waiting all day to tell you what happened."

I sat down at the table, feeling that I didn't really need another dose of news.

"I just had the feeling that I should run over and see how the Romanis survived the storm," Augusta was saying. "Why anyone would choose to live in that flimsy wagon, I'll never know. I was sure I'd find it turned over and the whole family dead or dying. Well, it wasn't that bad, but they did get a scare. Mr. Romani finally agreed to move his family into the cabin on the Abbots' property. Flora Abbot and I helped them get their things out of the wagon and into the house." Augusta shook her head. "Pitiful, what that family lives with. The children sleep right on the floor! Mrs. Romani doesn't have near enough furniture to set up in that cabin. I've been looking to see what I can spare. Maybe Emily Williams has something she could give."

"I'll mention it to her when I'm there this evening," I said. "I'm glad the Romanis are going to be in a house. I've worried about them—especially Maryanne. She's such a frail little thing."

"I'm surprised they're still here," Augusta said. "I never expected them to stay around this long. Never could understand why some people prefer to wander instead of getting their own land and living on it."

I preferred to turn the conversation away from the topic of land.

"I'm glad I decided to stay here this weekend," I said. "The roads are going to be bad after that rain. Sarah Jane had other plans, too, so it worked out fine. This will be my first Sunday morning in the North Branch church since school began."

"About time, too," Augusta replied. "I wouldn't leave *my* young man alone every weekend."

"He's hardly alone, Augusta," I protested. "Besides, we've been through all that. I'm not devoting my time to watching Elizabeth Lawton, or to running Len's life. He can take care of himself."

"You'll learn," Augusta predicted. "And you can remember that I told you so."

And if I don't, you'll remind me, I thought. Aloud, I said, "I do believe you'd enjoy being right about Elizabeth."

"I *am* right," she snapped, "and I *don't* enjoy it. This isn't the first time in my life I've watched a conniving female destroy a couple's plans. I don't want it to happen to you and Leonard."

"I believe the Lord brought us together, Augusta, and I don't think He'll allow anyone to come between us. You're worrying about the wrong thing this time."

"Have it your way," she said with a shrug. "All young women know more at twenty than they ever will again."

"I told Jerome we'd be over to see him," Len said when he came to get me on Saturday. "I'm sure he'll be able to advise us. But I don't see how we'll he able to keep Augusta from finding out about the will."

"It's ironic," I said. "Here I am worried about Augusta, and she's . . ." I caught myself before I finished the sentence, but Len didn't seem to notice. I wasn't about to tell him what Augusta was worrying over.

"Don't worry about it, Mabel," he said. "The Lord will work everything out. He knows that Augusta needs a home, and He won't forsake her."

"Len, have you thought about Mr. Grayson's interest in that property? Do you think he might try to work things around to his advantage?"

Len glanced at me. "You still don't trust him, do you?"

"I would feel better if he believed in something more solid than an 'unknown higher power,'" I admitted. "I guess I have no real reason not to trust him."

"I wish he knew the Lord as his Savior, too," Len agreed. "But in the meantime, I believe in the man's integrity and I'll continue to pray for him."

I knew Len was right, and I determined not to allow my prejudices to color my opinion of Mr. Grayson. We arrived at their house and were greeted loudly by Daniel.

"Hello, Mr. Williams! Hello, Miss O'Dell!" he boomed. "Papa says to come right in. He's waiting for you."

Mrs. Grayson came out to the porch. "I can't convince Daniel that people can hear him if he doesn't shout," she apologized as she held the door open. "Come in. Jerome is in his office."

She ushered us into a room furnished with a desk, bookcases, and a typewriter. It was very professional looking and a bit intimidating.

Jerome Grayson gave us a warm welcome. "Miss O'Dell, Len. Sit down. What can I do for you? I hope it's nothing serious; I'm not used to making appointments for my friends."

"I'm afraid it *is* serious, Mr. Grayson," I said. "We want you to see what we've found and tell us what we should do."

Len handed the packet of papers to him, and while Jerome read them, I looked around the room with interest. I hadn't seen so large a collection of books outside a library, and I was curious as to what this man might read. In addition to a number of law books, there seemed to be a lot of history and political science volumes. Surprisingly, I spotted some theology and other Christian topics, including Bunyan's *Pilgrim's Pro-*

gress. I was about to draw Len's attention to these when Mr. Grayson spoke.

"Is Miss Harris aware of this?"

I shook my head. "I didn't want her to know. I'm afraid she'll be completely crushed."

"Unless I'm mistaken, it will take more than this to crush that lady," Jerome said with a smile. "I agree with you, though. It is serious." He glanced again at the papers in his hand. "She obviously didn't know that her brother had married before he left, since she assured me that she was the only relative he had."

"I don't think the Gages know it, either," Len said. "Surely someone would have mentioned it when John died, or at least after Marcie died a few months later."

"Not necessarily," Jerome replied. "Perhaps her family wasn't in favor of the marriage and decided not to acknowledge it publicly, since both of them died within the year." He drummed his fingers on the desk and stared thoughtfully into the distance. "There is every possibility that the Gages are not aware of the will, however."

"I wish none of them needed to know," I commented. "But we can't pretend we never saw it."

"We could," Jerome replied, "but it would

hardly be the wise thing to do. This will was not witnessed and probably would not stand up in court. But there may be a properly executed document on file in the courthouse with the original deed. In that case, if Miss Harris should ever be inclined to sell, such a document would come to light when the deed was transferred. I think the shock to her would be more severe under those circumstances than if she were to be advised of your findings now."

"Oh, dear." I stared at him bleakly. "There's nothing we can do? Augusta is going to lose the home that's been in her family since 1790?"

"That shouldn't be a foregone conclusion," Jerome said. "There are several things we can do. I suggest we begin by tracking down the original deed. I assume it was transferred from father to son, since the claim was first made in 1790. If we find that John Harris was the owner in 1863, and there is no notarized copy of this will on file, then Miss Harris should be appraised of the existence of this paper and allowed to make her own decision as to whether she should honor her brother's wishes."

We were silent for a moment, then Len spoke. "Augusta has a strong sense of fairness," he said. "In light of the fact that

Marcie is no longer living, she might feel that the matter had taken care of itself. On the other hand, she could consider herself honor bound to abide by John's decision."

"You said there were several things we could do," I reminded Jerome. "What if you find that there *is* a signed and witnessed copy of the will? What happens then?"

"Augusta Harris would have the option of contesting the will. Under the circumstances, I would say that her chances of retaining the property are rather good. Of course, if the Gages realize what a valuable piece of real estate it is, there could be quite a fight."

"A fight!" I was stunned. "Between Augusta and the Gage family?"

"Actually, I was referring to a legal skirmish, not an armed battle," Jerome said with a smile. "I'm sure the Gages would do all they could to keep their inheritance intact."

Len spoke up suddenly. "I'm not!"

Jerome looked at him with surprise.

"You see," Len explained, "as Christians we don't feel that brother needs to go against brother in the law. There are better ways to solve our differences. I've never spoken with either the Gages or Augusta on this point, but I'm sure they'd say the same."

"You mean neither of them would contend

for what they thought was rightfully theirs?"

"I mean I don't think either of them would take the other to court and allow a judge to decide between them. They would reach a satisfactory settlement by praying and talking about it," Len replied.

Jerome shook his head in bewilderment. "I don't understand that. I'd expect a person in the right to demand a fair settlement, not give up his rights under the law."

"Christ didn't," Len said quietly.

"So I understand," Jerome replied drily. "And look where it got Him."

"Not a bad place to be, I'd say—" Len said with a grin—"on the right hand of the Father. But, Jerome, we aren't talking about people who have wronged each other. The Gages and the Harrises have been friends for years."

"I've seen friendships destroyed for far less than thousands of acres of prime forest . . . but you know these people better than I do. You may be right." He stood up and smiled. "We'll see, won't we? Now let's ask Myra if she has some coffee ready for us."

7

Quiet Before
The Tempest

LEN AND I RODE HOME IN SILENCE. WE had agreed with Jerome Grayson's suggestion that we say nothing to Augusta until a search had been made for the original deed. Jerome promised to make the trip to the county seat on Monday.

"You wouldn't believe the dirt I've shoveled out of this house," Augusta sputtered when I came in. "They're still working on that tree, and the wind was just right to blow all the sawdust under the doors. Even had to take the dishes out of the lower cupboards."

"I should have been here to help you," I said. "Why didn't you mention it before I left this morning?"

"You helped, all right," Augusta replied. "The best thing anyone can do for me when I'm cleaning is to stay out of the way. Did you have your supper?"

"Yes. I ate at Len's."

"Thought you would, so I didn't wait. I suppose he's glad you're going to be here for church tomorrow for a change."

"I think he is," I replied. "I'm looking forward to it. What time are you planning to leave in the morning?"

"Aren't you going with Len?" Augusta asked.

I shook my head. "He goes early to open up and get things ready. And I can't sit with him anyway." I laughed. "I hadn't thought about never being able to sit with my husband in church. I'll feel like a displaced person."

"There are many women who don't sit with their husbands in church," Augusta commented. "At least you'll know where yours is."

The first person I saw when we arrived Sunday morning was Elizabeth Lawton. The thought went through my mind that she obviously knew what time Len arrived and made it a point to be there. Immediately I was annoyed with myself for being suspicious. I determined to be friendly to Elizabeth, whether I felt like it or not, but as usual, she didn't make that an easy task.

"Good morning, Augusta," she said. She surveyed me coolly. "Mabel, how nice of you to grace us with your presence this morning. Did your friend—what's her name?—decide that you didn't need to make the trip home this weekend?"

Before I could think of a suitable retort, Elizabeth turned away.

"I feel sorry for her," Amelia Mathews's soft voice spoke beside me. "She's never had a home that she wanted to go back to. I suspect she's never had a friend like your Sarah Jane, either."

I turned toward her gratefully. "Sorrow isn't exactly what I feel toward Elizabeth. In spite of my best resolves, I always end up wanting to smack her. That's hardly a Christian attitude," I admitted ruefully.

"Understandable, though," Amelia laughed. "I'm glad to see you. How is your mother getting on?"

"Just fine, I assume. Pa said he would get word to me if I'm needed. I think both of them feel that things will go a lot smoother if I'm not there!"

It was time for church to begin, and I took my place beside Augusta. In spite of what had happened, I enjoyed the worship service. As we prayed, I thanked the Lord for His blessings: a good home, a wonderful family, and Len. The future looked bright.

When church was dismissed, I was surrounded by some of my children and their parents.

"I hadn't realized how long it's been since I've seen you," I said as I hugged Flora

Abbot. "Your girls are doing so well in school. Most of the time I can't even tell them apart!"

"Brace yourself," she said. "There are two more on the way." She laughed at the look on my face. "That's right. Dr. Mason says it's twins again."

"That's wonderful!" I exclaimed. "But why didn't Augusta tell me?"

"She doesn't know," Flora whispered. "Now you have something to tell her. There's not much that she doesn't know first."

There's something else she doesn't know, and I wish I didn't either, I thought.

I looked toward the door where Len had been shaking hands with people and saw that he and Jerome Grayson were talking. I wondered what they were planning, but I wouldn't have thought of joining them. Elizabeth, however, had no such compunctions. Under the pretense of taking care of the hymnals, she lingered close enough to overhear their conversation.

Any thoughts were interrupted by Len's mother, who was inviting Augusta for dinner. "There's no point in fixing a big meal just for yourself," she said.

"Done it most of my life," Augusta replied, "but I'll admit that it aids the digestion to have someone to talk to while I eat." She looked at me thoughtfully and added, "Even if it is a young one who doesn't think her elders know what they are talking about."

She looked significantly toward Elizabeth, but I pretended not to notice. I walked out to the buggy with them, and we waited for Mr. Williams and Len to close the church and join us. Watching Elizabeth walk toward home with the other Lawton children, I tried to tell myself that she must have some good traits. She attended church faithfully, even though her parents never came. But why? To hear the sermon or to see the preacher?

Mrs. Williams chattered about neighborhood happenings as we put dinner on the table. "There's a new baby at the Sawyers'," she reported. "Born yesterday. They named her Hope."

"I wondered why I didn't see Hannah and Teddy this morning," I said.

"They stayed with their aunt. She'll bring them back in time for school tomorrow."

"We won't be without a beginner class forever," I said. "The Abbots are expecting another set of twins. I wonder if I'll have as much trouble telling them apart as I've had with Rosie and Josie."

Augusta looked so surprised that I couldn't resist a chance to tease her. "How could you have missed a big news item like that,

Augusta? It isn't often that I get to tell you what's happening in North Branch."

"That's true," she admitted good-naturedly. "I guess you're entitled to share a surprise now and then."

Again I thought of the surprise I wasn't eager to share. We sat down to eat, and the conversation turned to other matters. When dinner was over, I began to clear the table.

"Are you too tired for a walk, Mabel?" Len asked.

"Why, no. I'd love to get out for a while." I smiled at him. "I need to have the cobwebs swept away."

"I'll help Emily," Augusta said. "You go along now."

"Better bring your coat," Len advised me. "It's getting nippy. I think we're skipping October this year and heading straight into winter."

We turned north toward the river and walked in silence for several minutes. The wind was cool, but the late fall sun was still warm enough to be comforting. Len tucked my hand in his pocket and looked down at me fondly.

"I'm not much good at expressing myself except in a sermon," he said. "You do know how much I care about you, don't you?"

"Of course I do, Len," I replied. "Words

aren't always necessary to let people know what you feel. I talk too much sometimes. I need you for balance."

"Well, I don't talk enough sometimes," Len offered. "I hold things inside that should be said." He paused, then added, "Mabel, do you plan to continue teaching after we're married?"

"Why, I hadn't thought of not teaching. I enjoy it so much, and besides, we could . . ."

"Use the money?" Len finished for me. "I know I can't provide for you as I would like to on a preacher's salary, but I was hoping that with the farm, we'd get along all right."

"We will, Len," I said. "I wasn't even thinking about what you might prefer. I just love my school teaching so much that I don't consider it work."

"If I asked you not to teach because of my pride, that would be pretty selfish," Len admitted. "It would be the same as having you ask me to choose another profession so that we could live better."

"I don't want to live better," I stated emphatically. "I accepted you for what you are. More than anything, I want you to do the Lord's will and be happy."

"Thank you, Mabel. I appreciate that. What would you think of continuing to teach at your school until we have children of our own? Would that be satisfactory?"

"Oh, Len!" I exclaimed. "That would be perfect! Are you sure that's the way you want it?"

"I can live with that." He grinned. "I hope all our problems are this easy to solve."

We reached a clearing on the edge of Augusta's property and sat down on a rail fence overlooking the river.

"Jerome is going to the county seat in the morning," Len said. "He has other business besides the Harris property, and he asked if I'd like to go along. I could look through the records while he takes care of other things."

"Are you going?"

Len nodded. "It'll be a good opportunity to spend some time with him. Lately, he's been questioning me about what we believe. And I'm anxious to know about the deed, too. One way or another, a decision has to be made."

"I hope we're doing the right thing," I said. "Keeping those papers from Augusta, I mean. When it comes right down to it, it's really none of our business, is it?"

"I suppose not," Len said slowly. "But I'm sure Augusta is going to be grateful for any help she can get in taking care of this problem. The more we know, the better we'll be able to help her."

"If there's no will, the whole thing will be

up to her. If there is one, the Gages will be involved. I don't know which way I hope it will go."

"It won't be easy, either way," Len agreed.

We watched a pair of squirrels rustling through the leaves and carrying nuts up the trees. I shivered as I thought of the long, cold winter ahead.

"Are you chilly?" Len asked. "It's time to start back anyway. I need to get ready for the evening service. Are you planning to come?"

"Where else would I go?" I said. "Hurry up. I'll race you to the road."

"No fair," Len complained when we stopped to catch a breath. "You had a head start."

"That's what Sarah Jane always says. No one will admit that I can run faster than most people."

"You just don't have as much to carry," Len said. "Try carrying seventy extra pounds and see who wins."

Elizabeth was at the evening service.

"I didn't expect to see her here," I said to Augusta. "Doesn't she go back to her boarding place in town on Sunday afternoon?"

"Once in a while she waits till Monday morning," Augusta answered, "especially during the summer when you aren't here."

Church didn't last long on Sunday night,

but it was dark when we finally locked the door. Len took us home.

"I don't know what time we'll get back tomorrow evening," he said. "You won't be needing Regal for anything, will you?"

I shook my head.

"Then I'll take our rig. I'll see you Tuesday. If you do need to get home, my pa will see that you have a way."

"It's early yet," I said. "Ma isn't due for at least three weeks."

"Where is he off to?" Augusta wanted to know when we were inside.

"With Mr. Grayson," I replied. "They have some business to look into."

For some reason Augusta didn't persist in her questioning, and I retreated thankfully to my room to get ready for bed.

8
The Tempest Breaks

I WAS PUTTING LESSONS ON THE BOARD MONday morning when I became aware that a heated argument was taking place outside my window. With a sigh I put the chalk down and went out to see what the problem was. Julie Ann Lawton and Edward Alexander were standing toe to toe.

"That's a lie!" Edward shouted.

"Don't you call my pa a liar!" Julie Ann bellowed, giving Edward a push. To my surprise, the usually mild-mannered Edward grabbed Julie Ann by the hair. At that point, George Elliot took one child in each hand and held them at arm's length. Julie Ann was red faced with anger, and Edward was crying with rage.

"I thought I'd better separate them before they killed each other," George said.

"Thank you, George. What in the world started all this?"

"Her pa said that my pa started the fire in the school, and that's a lie!" Edward shouted. "A great, big lie!"

" 'Tis not," Julie Ann retorted. "My pa knows, 'cause he saw your pa running away from school."

"This is not the way to prove anything," I said firmly. "Both of you go and sit on the steps until you cool off. We'll talk about this later."

I had hoped to uncover interesting facts about the school and community, not dig up old resentments and rumors. When the bell rang, everyone filed in quietly. After the opening exercises, the children waited expectantly for me to say something about the morning's unusual beginning.

"We want to have a centennial pageant," I said, "but not if people are going to be hurt because of it. I think we should have some rules about the kinds of things that will be included. What do we want to know about the school?"

"Who came here," Jamie suggested.

"Who all the teachers were," Prudence offered, "and maybe which one stayed the longest."

Many other ideas were expressed, and then I said, "All right, these are facts people in the valley may remember. There are a lot of stories connected with the school that will not injure anyone's reputation if they are repeated. These are what we want to hear."

"But the school *did* burn," Carrie pointed out.

"That's true," I replied. "And the fact can be included. But no one was ever proven responsible according to the school records, and we'll leave it at that. We'll report only what we *know*."

"My pa knows," Julie Anne muttered, and Edward glared at her.

"Julie Ann," I said sternly, "we have heard the last word on the subject. Do you understand?"

She nodded reluctantly, and we went on to other things. I kept an eye on the two combatants the rest of the day, but they stayed a reasonable distance apart. As soon as school was dismissed, I made my way over to see Mrs. Williams.

"I'm not surprised," she said when I related the story. "There's not been any love lost between the Alexanders and Cy Lawton since he arrived here. As I recall, the Lawtons came during the winter of '74, when Elizabeth was about five. Cyrus wanted her to go into the first grade, but Philip Alexander—Edward's grandfather—was president of the school board, and he ruled that Elizabeth should stay in the beginners' class the rest of the year. Apparently Cy has held that against the Alexanders all these years."

"You think he made up the story to discredit the family?"

"It wouldn't surprise me. Our girls were in school with Paul Alexander. He was one of the nicest boys in school—quiet and easygoing, just like Edward is. Certainly not the type to burn down the schoolhouse."

"I thought we were headed for another Civil War," I sighed. "I was tempted to quit the whole project."

"Every community has its little rumors and intrigues, especially when families have been a part of it for a hundred years," Mrs. Williams said. "When people start searching their memories, they are bound to come to mind."

"Well, I hope I'm not sorry we started this." I rose to leave. "What time do you expect Len?"

"I think they were planning to spend the day," Mrs. Williams replied. "It will probably be well after dark before they get here."

I went home to find Augusta surveying her well-filled woodshed with satisfaction. "Who'd have believed that one tree would have that much firewood?" she marveled. "I sent a load to the Romanis, and Hiram took a bunch of kindling. There's still enough here to keep us going far into the winter."

"I see they got the well house back up," I

remarked. "Was it damaged too much?"

"Not at all. When Pa put something together, he meant it to stay that way until the end of time. Hiram just had to push it up straight and seal the bottom. This place will outlast all of us."

I certainly hope so, I thought, and went in to work on my lessons.

I had not had time to hang up my coat the following day when Mrs. Williams hurried into the classroom.

"Mabel, has Len been here this morning?" she asked.

"Why, no," I answered. "I just this minute got here. Didn't he come home last night?"

"No, he didn't. But Regal did."

"You mean the horse came home alone?" I gasped.

She nodded. "Pa found him in his stall this morning. There's no sign of the buggy or Len. Pa's going to set out looking for him if you haven't seen him. Oh, dear. I hope there hasn't been an accident."

She hurried out, and I stared after her in shock. I couldn't leave the children unattended, nor would I be any help in searching for Len. I would have to carry on until news came.

When the children arrived, I went out to

speak to the Graysons. "Did your father come home last night, Serena?" I asked.

"No, ma'am," she replied. "He didn't intend to. He took the train from Riverdale to meet someone, and he'll be home later today."

"Elizabeth didn't come home, neither," Julie Ann put in.

"What does that have to do with anything?" I snapped. I was tired of hearing Julie Anne's reports from home, and I was terribly worried about Len.

"She was with 'em," Julie Ann stated. "She's on vacation from her job this week, and Pa's awful upset because they didn't get back."

Carrie scowled at her, but Julie Anne continued, undaunted. "Pa says he'll have a word with *that* young man. He'll probably make Mr. Williams marry Elizabeth!"

I could understand why Edward had been ready to snatch this child bald. "That's enough, Julie Ann. Everyone line up to come inside, please."

I walked stiffly into the schoolroom and rang the bell for the opening of the day. After assigning the morning lessons and enlisting Prudence and Elsie to hear the little ones read, I hovered near the window where I could watch the road.

Len must have known Sunday night that Elizabeth was going to the county seat with them. Why hadn't he told me? And what had she gone for? If Jerome Grayson had gone someplace else, that meant Len and Elizabeth would travel back alone. But where were they now? How could Len have *done* this?

Serena's voice broke into my whirling thoughts. "Miss O'Dell? I think it's time for recess." I slowly brought her into focus and nodded. "All right. Go."

The children rose quietly, casting sidelong glances at me as they filed out. I had to pull myself together and live out this day. Before evening, I realized, everyone in North Branch would know that Leonard Williams and Elizabeth Lawton had left together yesterday and had not yet returned. I forced myself to push the matter out of my mind and concentrate on schoolwork. I would not go near that window again.

Recess over, the children came back in. We proceeded at once with a scheduled spelldown, and they seemed relieved to see that I was paying attention to them. I even joined in the laughter when Hannah spelled "believe" b-e-l-e-a-v-e, but my heart was definitely not in it.

Shortly before noontime, Len came driving

into the school yard—alone. I dismissed the children for dinner, and they grabbed their lunch pails and sidled past him in the doorway. Julie Ann threw a smug look in my direction, and I clutched my chair to keep from going after her. I had never disliked a child in my life, but I was coming mighty close to losing what little affection I had for this one.

I stood still as Len approached the desk.

"I was concerned about you," I said evenly.

"I know. I'm sorry. Regal was—got loose. I had to wait until this morning to hire a horse. There was no way to let you or Ma know what had happened."

I watched as he awkwardly shifted his hat from hand to hand. Finally, he cleared his throat.

"Do you want to know what we found?"

"Of course."

"The property was in John Harris's name, and there is a witnessed will on file. That means the Gages—and Augusta—will have to be told."

I made no reply, and Len watched me warily.

"Aren't you going to say something?"

"Len, why didn't you tell me that Elizabeth Lawton was going with you?"

He looked uncomfortable. "I know how you

feel about Elizabeth," he said timidly. "I didn't think you'd want to know."

"You mean you thought I wouldn't find out? How many other things are you planning to keep from me?"

"I don't intend to keep anything—"

"Never mind," I interrupted. "You were right. I don't want to know." I walked past him and out to the school yard, leaving Len to see himself to the door.

9

Sarah Jane to
The Rescue

B Y THE TIME THE DAY ENDED, I HAD A
pounding headache.

"I don't want any supper, Augusta," I told her when I reached home. "I'm going to lie down until this pain stops."

She nodded, and the grim look on her face told me that she knew about Len and Elizabeth. To her credit, she refrained from saying "I told you so."

In my room, I dropped my books on the desk and flung myself across the bed, too angry to cry. Sooner or later I knew I would have to face Len and break our engagement, but I was in no shape to go through that right now. I tried to sort out my tangled feelings. Perhaps the most horrifying thought was that Cy Lawton would make trouble for Len. Whether he felt he had a legitimate case or not, he was sure to press his advantage. Elizabeth *had* left with Len, and they had not returned until the following day. Those facts would be hard to refute.

For the first time in my life, I seemed

unable to pray about a problem. I could not imagine the end of the world being more bleak.

Len arrived right after suppertime, and Augusta came to my door. "Len is here. Do you want to come out?"

"No."

She turned and went back to the kitchen. "She's resting, Len. She won't be out this evening."

I couldn't hear Len's reply, but the outside door closed, and the house was quiet. I fell into an uneasy sleep, awoke later, and undressed for bed. I might as well not have bothered, because I didn't go to sleep again.

When I heard Augusta stirring, I went out to help with breakfast.

"You're going to school this morning?" she asked me.

"Yes. I can't spend the rest of my life in bed."

"You look like something the cat wouldn't have," Augusta commented. "I hope you're going to eat some breakfast."

"I feel like something the cat already had," I replied. "And the only reason I'm eating breakfast is because I don't want to fall in a heap before the day is over."

The children had the good sense to give me plenty of room, and the morning dragged on uneventfully. Even Julie Ann was silent; a circumstance which probably saved her from mortal injury.

About an hour before dismissal time, I reached a decision. I would go to see Sarah Jane.

"Children, I have something to take care of this afternoon. I'm going to let you leave early. Take the lessons you haven't completed home with you, and I'll expect finished work on my desk tomorrow morning."

Faces brightened, and the children lost no time getting books and papers together and charging out of the building. I was close on the heels of the last child to leave.

Len didn't hear me approach the barn, and he jumped when I spoke to him.

"May I please take Regal and the buggy for a few hours?"

"Of course. Is everything all right?" he asked anxiously. "Did you hear from home?"

"Everything is fine. I have an errand to take care of."

He hurried to bring Regal out and hitch him to the buggy. "If you had let me know I could have met you at school. You needn't have walked over." He helped me up into the seat. "Mabel, please . . ."

The look of pain and bewilderment on his face almost unnerved me. I wanted to jump down and throw my arms around his neck, but I hardened my heart.

"*I'll* be home before dark," I said pointedly, and drove out of the yard without looking back. I arrived in Edenville before Sarah Jane had left her school.

"Sarah Jane," I said as I marched to the front of the room, "tell me that there is still something funny about life."

She looked startled, then sat back in her chair and raised one eyebrow.

"Well, for starters, you have your hat on sideways."

I grabbed my hat and threw it on the front desk, then promptly sat on it.

Alarm registered on her face. "Mabel, have you had bad news from home?"

"No, I haven't," I snapped. "Why is everyone concerned about Ma when I'm the one that's in trouble?"

She looked relieved. "Somehow I'm not surprised to hear that. It's a little like reading last week's newspaper."

"Sarah Jane, can you be serious for once in your life?"

"Mabel, you came storming in here in the middle of a Wednesday afternoon with your hat on sideways and asked if life is funny. Now, I don't suppose you want to tell me what's going on?"

"I'm not going to marry Len."

She took that in. "Oh, dear. And I was so looking forward to standing up with you. I was planning on a new dress."

"Sarah Jane!" I wailed.

"All right, all right. If I fell apart with sorrow, you'd start to howl. I can get more out of you if you're mad. Now, start at the beginning." She came around and sat down on the desk next to me. "And get off your hat."

I stood up, and she began to punch my hat back into shape.

"I don't know where to begin," I said.

"You'd better start somewhere, unless you intend to spend the night," Sarah Jane suggested.

At that, I burst into tears, and she put her arms around me.

"I know; it has to be awful. Why don't you give me the worst thing first?"

"Leonard will probably have to marry Elizabeth," I sobbed.

Sarah Jane took out a handkerchief. "Here. You're getting your front all wet. Was this her idea, or his?"

"Her father's."

"And I thought the days of arranged marriages were past. What's the next worst thing?" she continued.

"Len didn't tell me she was going!"

Sarah Jane patted my hand. "Mabel, I seem to be missing a vital link in this story. What would you think of starting at the top and working your way back down?"

I gulped and began with the fact that Len had accompanied Jerome to Springdale on Monday, that he had not returned until Tuesday noon, and that I'd learned from a schoolchild that Elizabeth had been with him.

"Sounds like a good plot for a melodrama," Sarah Jane said. "So what was Len's explanation?"

"He didn't give me one."

"You mean he came riding in with a strange horse, eighteen hours late, and didn't tell you why?"

"I told him I didn't want to know."

"Ah." Sarah Jane grinned. "Now *that's* the Mabel I know and love. You'd rather imagine a terrible disaster than listen to a logical explanation."

"What logical explanation could there possibly be?" I demanded hotly. "He took her to Springdale for . . . for whatever reason—and they came back alone. What else do I need to know?"

"Several things come to mind," Sarah Jane said. "If it were my fiancé, I'd want to know how the horse got away. I'd also ask how Elizabeth knew he was going to Springdale, and what reason she gave for needing to tag along. Assuming, of course, that she made the arrangements."

"I can't even assume that," I retorted bitterly.

"In other words," Sarah Jane supplied, "you don't trust Len."

I heard myself saying to Augusta, *If I can't trust him, I have no business planning to marry him.* I shifted uncomfortably on the desk. "It takes two people to make arrangements like that," I muttered.

"Didn't you say that Jerome was along? Maybe Elizabeth appealed to him without Len knowing it. Jerome isn't acquainted with her wicked ways yet; he might not have realized that she had anything more devious in mind than a day's shopping trip."

"I never thought of that."

"You are nosing up the wrong trail, my girl," Sarah Jane stated. "Follow that horse—*there* is the key to this whole web of intrigue."

"You're probably right," I said. "But I've never had a whole lot of luck conversing with horses. How do I get Regal to talk?"

"Ask Len, Mabel. You didn't give him a chance to tell you what *he* knew."

I thought it over for a moment. "Suppose what you say is true. We still have the possibility of Cy Lawton making trouble for Len. Not to mention the busybodies who like nothing better than to chew on a good story."

"You're living with the master body of the lot," Sarah Jane reminded me. "Augusta will set the village straight before the next Sabbath. As for Cy Lawton, if what I suspect is so, you won't hear anymore out of him."

I looked at Sarah Jane dubiously. "What do you suspect?"

"Mabel, you'll have to swallow your pride and talk this whole thing over with Len. I'd ask you to stay and have supper with me, but you need to get back before dark." She grinned. "Unless you want the busybodies chewing on you."

We walked out to the buggy together, and I hugged her. "I don't know what I'd ever do without you, Sarah Jane. You always manage to turn things right side up for me."

"That's true," she nodded. "If I didn't intervene, you'd spend half your life spinning around on your ear. Now, get. I'll see you Friday. And don't forget to wash my handkerchief."

She waved good-bye, and I turned Regal's head toward home. I had to admit my foolish pride had blown the whole incident out of proportion. If I had only allowed Len to tell me about it, I could have avoided one giant headache. Suddenly I realized that my pain was gone, and I was starving. I urged Regal to go faster, and we were back in North Branch before the sun went down.

Len saw me coming and was standing by the porch when I stopped the buggy. He put out his hand to help me down, but I held out both arms. He caught me and held me close.

"I'm sorry, Len. I should have let you explain what happened—but you don't have to tell me anything at all. I trust you."

"But I want to tell you," he said. "Come and have supper, then we'll talk."

Later, as we walked slowly toward home, Len unfolded his story.

"Elizabeth overheard Jerome ask me to go to Springdale with him, so after I left the church, she asked him if she could ride along. I didn't know until we were on the way that Jerome wouldn't be coming back with us."

Once again, Sarah Jane is proven right, I thought.

"I didn't see her all day," he continued, "but when I got back to the place we were to meet, Regal was gone. I looked that town over till dark, and by that time, the livery stable was closed. There was nothing to do but get rooms for the night. Elizabeth stayed at a boarding house, and I stayed in the hotel. In the morning I hired a horse and picked her up." Len paused. "I guess her conscience was starting to hurt because she admitted that she had turned Regal loose and started him for home."

"Oh, Len! No!" I gasped. Then I shook my head. "It won't surprise Augusta any. She'll say it's just the kind of trick she would expect that girl to pull. I'm surprised you didn't put her out on the road and let her walk home."

"Don't think I wasn't tempted," Len declared. "If I'd found out about the horse before we left town, I'd have left her there and sent her pa back to get her. I did let her know that if she failed to tell her father exactly what happened, I'd be over there to tell him myself."

"Len, I think Augusta deserves to know what happened," I said when we reached the house. "I haven't been very decent to her lately."

We told her the story in brief, and her reaction to Elizabeth's scheming was just as I'd predicted. Then Augusta rose to get ready for bed.

"I hope whatever business you had to take care of was worth all that," she said. "This

98

has been one dismal place the last two days."

We looked at each other after she had left.

"Poor Augusta," Len said. "She doesn't know half the story about that trip. I'm afraid 'dismal' isn't going to cover it when we tell her about those papers." He sighed. "We'll talk more tomorrow. It's sure to be a better day than this one has been."

10

Augusta Gets
The News

THE CHILDREN KEPT A WARY EYE ON ME
when they arrived the next morning. I
had been acting rather strangely, and
I was sure that all but the very littlest ones
knew what had taken place. Today I would
have welcomed news from the Lawton house
that Elizabeth had felt her father's wrath,
but neither Carrie nor Julie Anne said anything in my hearing.

Edward, however, had information that he
was anxious to impart, and I had difficulty
restraining him until morning prayers were
over.

"My pa knows who set fire to the school!"
he exclaimed, "but he won't tell because it
wouldn't serve any good purpose!" He looked
triumphantly at Julie Ann, who turned away
and stared out the window. "But he remembers something else that could be included in
our pageant."

"That's fine, Edward. What is it?"

"The school board hired a man named
Robert Rosswell to rebuild the schoolhouse

in 1875. Pa says Mr. Rosswell made a new cornerstone and let everyone who was in school that year put something inside it. Then he set it in the southwest corner. Pa said it wasn't to be opened until one hundred years later."

"That will be 1975!" Jamie said. "There won't be any of us around to see."

Thank heaven for that, I thought. I couldn't cope with any more buried treasure at the moment. But aloud, I said, "Some people live to be very old. Let's figure out how many years that is from now. Joel, come and put it on the board for us."

Joel came up and wrote *1975-1892=83.* The children stared at the number silently.

"That's *forever,*" Hannah breathed.

"Not quite," I laughed. "Do you know how to find out how old you'll be in eighty-three years?"

"We can subtract the year we were born from 1975," Serena suggested.

"It would be faster to add how old you are now to eighty-three." Prudence offered.

I nodded. "It will work either way. Why don't you figure it out?"

All was quiet as the children concentrated on their calculations.

"I'll never make it," George announced. "I'll be ninety-seven years old!"

"I'll be ninety-five," Joel sighed. "I wish the school had burned fifty years earlier. If it was going to burn at all," he added hastily when I looked at him.

We discovered that the youngest child would be eighty-nine years old in 1975.

"How about you, Miss O'Dell? How old will you be in 1975?" Toby wanted to know.

"Over one hundred years," I said. "I rather doubt that I'll be here for the opening."

They looked at me as though they could see me aging before their eyes. Finally Prudence broke the silence.

"Well, whoever is still alive can meet here at the school and get their grandchildren to whack the cornerstone open." She turned to Edward. "Did your pa tell you what he put in there?"

Edward blushed. "A valentine from his girl friend. He wouldn't tell me who she was—just that it wasn't my ma!"

The children laughed, and Elsie's eyes sparkled.

"When we have our pageant, Edward's pa will be here, and maybe his girl friend. Someone might tell us who it was!" she exclaimed.

I wondered again if this had been a wise project to begin. We turned our attention to the daily lessons, and as the children worked, I thought of the revelation that lay ahead for Augusta.

Len and I wanted Jerome to be there when we told about her brother's marriage and the will. When we approached him that evening, Jerome agreed that Augusta would need advice, and he was willing to help her if she wanted him to.

"I'm not sure that Miss Harris will respond too kindly to my assistance, since I've twice made an offer to buy her property," he said. "One reason I wanted Len to search for the papers was to allay her suspicions that I might have engineered the find."

"There is a reason that the Lord allows circumstances to come into our lives," Len said. "That tree could have gone over years ago, or it could have fallen the other way. I believe that all this has happened now to touch individual lives, just as God planned."

Jerome regarded Len thoughtfully, but he made no comment. Since I would be going home this weekend, we decided to meet on Monday evening and break the news to Augusta.

"We'll let her decide when and how to inform the Gages," Jerome suggested. "It will be up to them to make the arrangements for her future welfare." He paused. "I hope they don't consider moving her out of her home. They could legally do so."

Len looked at him in astonishment. "Neither old Mrs. Gage nor Frank would ever consider anything like that!"

"Your Bible says that the love of money is the root of all evil," Jerome responded. "The Gage family stands to come into a goodly portion of those roots. I'd be very surprised if greed doesn't enter the picture someplace."

Len shook his head. "I think I know Frank better than that. I'll be very surprised if it *does*."

"Jerome Grayson has a hard time believing that the Golden Rule really works when it comes down to specific cases," I said to Sarah Jane as we rode home on Friday.

"He probably hasn't had a lot of opportunity to see it in action," Sarah Jane replied. "Things can get pretty sticky when there's money involved. Now for instance, if I had ten dollars, I'd be happy to see that you had half. But if it got into the thousands, I might have to give it a little thought."

"Not me," I said. "You're welcome to anything I have."

"Safe offer," Sarah Jane replied. "Your worldly possessions are no greater than mine. But I'll settle for my handkerchief. You did wash it, didn't you?"

"Augusta did." I sighed. "I'm not looking forward to Monday. I don't know what the news is going to do to her."

"She's a strong lady. I don't imagine she'll clap her hands for joy, but I don't think she'll faint, either."

"Mrs. Williams thinks that Augusta had her eye on Frank Gage's uncle when they were in school. Do you ever wonder how things might have turned out if just a few details had been different?"

"I've given it some thought," Sarah Jane admitted. "Especially since I had a letter from Thomas yesterday saying that Russ Bradley is engaged."

"Who to?"

"To whom," Sarah Jane corrected. She grinned. "You really *have* had a hard week."

"You startled me," I defended myself. "Who is Russ going to marry?"

"Your friend Clarice Owens—who else? Don't ever let anyone tell you that persistence doesn't pay. That girl was *determined.*"

I let this sink in, remembering my struggle to overcome my hostility toward Clarice and win at least a grudging acceptance from her.

When I didn't say anything, Sarah Jane inquired, "Are you having second thoughts about turning him down?"

"Never," I said definitely. "I was thinking about her. You know, she'll look more at home in that elegant place than I ever could. How could I manage a house full of servants?"

"I'd be willing to give it my best shot," Sarah Jane mused. "It's not likely to be one of my problems, either. Thomas is a dear, but he didn't choose wealthy ancestors, and he's certainly no financial wizard. I got as high a grade in math as he did. That's not saying a lot for either of us."

We rounded a curve in the road, and the Clarks' lane came into sight. "Are you going to tell your folks that you almost came back to live out your last days on the old home-place?" asked Sarah Jane.

"Not yet," I replied. "I'm afraid it would upset Ma. They think I've finally gotten past my foolish years, and I hate to disillusion them."

"Your secret is safe with me," Sarah Jane laughed.

I stopped the buggy in front of her gate, and she took her things out.

"I'll come by later to see how your ma is," she promised. "It won't be much longer now, will it?"

"This is the month. I'll be glad when it's over, and so will she, I'm sure."

Reuben and Jennie were visiting with young Jacob, and I was glad to see them.

"Jacob will have an aunt younger than he is to boss around," I commented.

"Aunt?" Reuben said. "He might have an uncle he can clobber."

"You'll never convince Mabel of that," Pa put in, smiling at me.

"When are you getting married, Mabel?" Jennie asked.

"We haven't decided on a date yet. Possibly before school starts next fall, if we can get a house ready by then."

"That will be our last wedding," Ma said. Then she laughed and added, "For eighteen or twenty years, anyway."

The weekend was a quiet one, and as I was leaving I reminded Pa to send word to me at once if the baby came.

"Three weeks yet, at least," he predicted. "But don't worry. You'll know, all right."

"I'm not going to have time to worry over Ma and the new baby," I said to Sarah Jane on the way back to North Branch. "Who knows what I'll have on my hands after we talk to Augusta tomorrow. I've really become very fond of her and I don't like to see her upset."

Augusta was surprised when Jerome

Grayson came in with Len after supper Monday, but she greeted him cordially enough. "I haven't changed my mind, Mr. Grayson," she said. "I hope you aren't counting on Len's help to convince me."

"No, Miss Harris. I've come for another reason this time. There is a legal matter that is going to need your attention, and I told Len that I'd be glad to assist you if you wish."

"Can't think of any reason why I'd need a lawyer," Augusta responded. "Always been able to take care of my own business. What is this matter, anyhow?"

"Perhaps Mabel should tell you how the whole thing came to light," Len suggested.

Augusta looked questioningly at me, and I began the story of the Elliot boys finding the box under the well house and bringing the papers to me. Jerome took the papers out and placed them on the table.

"This is a copy of the deed to this property," he explained, "and with it, a copy of your brother John's will."

We waited silently as Augusta read the handwritten page. Her face paled, but there was no indication of surprise or shock.

"So. John did marry her before he left. There's no question about that, I suppose?" She looked at Jerome.

"None at all," he replied. "I saw the marriage record. As to the will, in a case where this much money and property is at stake, you would not be faulted for challenging it. It's possible that the Gages knew no more about the marriage than your mother and you did."

He paused, but Augusta said nothing, so he continued. "If you wish to contest the will, the Gages must be informed so that they can retain legal counsel. In any event, they need to be told—unless, of course, you choose to destroy this paper and carry on as though it had never existed."

"You mean that's an option?" Augusta asked.

"And more commonly pursued than you might suspect. It was by accident that this came to anyone's attention. Had it not been for the storm, it quite possibly would never have been found."

The room was silent as Augusta walked to the window and stared out. Then she turned and said, "Mr. Grayson, I would like to hire your services."

11

Jerome Grayson
Gets a Surprise

I DON'T KNOW WHAT I EXPECTED, BUT IT wasn't that," I said to Len after Jerome had left, and Augusta had gone to her room. "Did it sound to you as though she might consider contesting the will?"

"It's hard to tell what she may have in mind to do about it," Len replied. "This has been a pretty big shock. She probably doesn't know herself."

But it was obvious the next morning that Augusta *did* have a plan. When I inquired, she replied that she had slept well and would go about her daily duties as usual. No, she wasn't worried about her future. Mr. Grayson would return this afternoon, and she intended to instruct him as to her wishes in the matter.

I left for school with no idea what her wishes might be. I remembered her emphatic statement to Jerome that there would be a Harris on the land as long as she lived, and Augusta did not change her mind easily.

Jerome met me on the road after school

was dismissed, and we walked toward home together. "Miss Harris wanted both you and Len to be there when we discussed this matter today," he explained. "Len is already there, doing some work for her."

"Have you any idea what she might be planning?" I asked.

Jerome shook his head. "Not a clue. I'm not even sure that she knows the extent of her holdings, but I do know that she feels strongly about family ties to the land." He glanced at me. "I know what you and Len believe, but I wouldn't place great odds on that outcome. People tend to temper their ideals when large amounts of money are involved."

I wanted to tell him that Christian attitudes went deeper than mere ideals, but I didn't know how to explain it.

Len waved as we neared the house, and Augusta greeted us cheerfully at the door. She had prepared tea and hot gingerbread, and the kitchen was warm and cozy on a nippy, November afternoon.

"Len has been mulching my trees and bushes," Augusta said. "Wouldn't be surprised if it snowed any day now. Can't remember when we've had such an early fall," she looked around the table at each of us. "Guess you aren't interested in talking about the weather, are you?"

"You've not had much time to make up your mind," Jerome said. "Considering the number of years that have already gone by, a few more days won't make a difference."

"Don't need more time," Augusta replied. "My mind was made up last night. Mr. Grayson, I want you to draw up whatever papers are necessary to transfer the Harris property to Frank Gage."

Jerome cleared his throat. "Miss Harris, are you aware of the magnitude of the area this deed encompasses? Even if it were all farmland, it would be of great value, but considering the worth of the timber, you are probably in possession of the richest acres in this part of Michigan. I would advise you to act with great restraint."

"There could be a pot of gold under every tree, and it still wouldn't be mine," Augusta snapped. "I fail to see what the value of the place has to do with its rightful disposition."

"You did ask me to represent you," Jerome replied. "I'd be remiss if I didn't present every side of the issue before you make a final decision. Have you considered what your options will be if Mr. Gage asks you to move to another location? Remember, too, that you are a very independent lady. How will you adjust to reliance upon the Gage family for your livelihood?"

Augusta looked surprised. "Mr. Grayson, my reliance is totally upon the Lord. However He chooses to take care of me is acceptable." She looked down at her hands folded in her lap. "I'll admit that it would be difficult to give up my home. I was born here and expected to die here." She thrust out her chin defiantly. "But I'm not so attached to any earthly thing that I couldn't live without it. As to the monetary value of the land, what would I do with more than I have? No, Mr. Grayson. I thank you for your concern, but my mind is made up. We'll abide by John's wishes."

Jerome looked as though he would like to argue the point further, but he said no more.

Augusta turned to Len. "How does the holly look, Len? I'd like to have lots of it to decorate the church for Christmas."

"It's thick," Len replied. "The berries are beginning to get red. They should be just right by December. There's enough for Mabel to use at school for the pageant, too."

"Good," Augusta said. "That should be an interesting program. Imagine! One hundred years of school in the same spot. That first building went up two years after my grandfather arrived here. Only the Elliots, the Gages, and the Harrises were here then.

Don't think the Williams family arrived until 1800 something. My father said they had kitchen schools until there were too many children to crowd together."

I thought about the huge kitchen at the Gages', with the fireplace big enough to stand in.

Augusta continued, "The Gages had the biggest place, and that was the last home school. They considered naming the new one after the family, but old Mr. Gage said no, it should be called by the county name. That held until more schools were built, then it took the branch name, the North Branch of the Chippewa River."

Jerome Grayson had been taking all this in silently, obviously wondering how Augusta could reminisce about community history when she was about to sign away a fortune. Finally he rose and reached for his hat.

"If this is your final consideration, Miss Harris, I'll prepare the necessary papers for you and Mr. Gage to sign. You may arrange a meeting with him at your convenience."

" 'Never put off until tomorrow what you can do today,' " Augusta quoted. "There's no reason why we couldn't go over there tonight. Matter of fact, I told them we'd be calling. Didn't tell 'em why, though." Her eyes twinkled. "That will be a surprise."

Jerome's look said that indeed it would, and he left, obviously puzzled by the unusual behavior of this woman.

"I must be going too," Len said. "It's time to help Pa with the chores."

"Come back for supper," Augusta told him. "We'll go over together."

I retreated to my room to work on my lessons, but found myself staring out the window at the old well house. What a chain of events hung on a strong wind!

If the Gages were surprised to see all of us troop into their house, they didn't show it. We were treated warmly and led over to chairs by the big fireplace. Grandmother Gage watched with interest as we seated ourselves and Dorcas offered us coffee.

"I don't believe I know this young man, Dorcas," old Mrs. Gage said. "Is he new in the area?"

"Yes, Mother," Dorcas replied. "This is Jerome Grayson. He's bought the old Tyler place."

Mrs. Gage nodded and turned her attention to me. "I hear you and the children are looking into the history of the school. You may dig up some things that people would rather remained buried."

"We aren't looking for personal items, Mrs.

Gage," I replied. "We just want historical facts about North Branch."

"All history is personal to someone," she remarked. "But I like what you're doing. It will be an interesting evening."

So will this one, I thought, settling back in my chair.

After a few moments of conversation, Augusta turned to Frank Gage. "We have some business to take care of, Frank," she said. "I'll let Mr. Grayson explain it to you."

Jerome produced the will, the deed, and the papers that he had prepared for the transfer. When the story was told, there was silence in the kitchen.

Finally Frank spoke. "Did you know that John and Marcie had married, Ma?"

Mrs. Gage shook her head. "No, but I'm not surprised. John asked permission to marry her the year before he left, but her pa and I thought she wasn't old enough. We told them to wait until she was nineteen, but John had to leave for the war. Apparently they decided to marry before he went and tell us about it when he returned."

"Of course, he didn't come back," Frank put in, "and Marcie died of lung fever the same winter. If it hadn't been for the storm, chances are we would never have known."

"We know now," Augusta said briskly, "so

116

we might as well finish up what we came to do."

"What did you come to do, Augusta?" Frank inquired.

"Why, transfer the deed to you, of course," Augusta replied. "The title goes to Marcie's heirs, and all of you are her family."

"We'll just need your signature here, Mr. Gage," Jerome said. "I'll see that the papers are filed at once."

Frank Gage shook his head. "I don't want it."

"I beg your pardon?"

"I don't want it," Frank repeated. "I've no right to the Harris property. I have all the land I need. And I certainly wouldn't take Augusta's house away from her."

Jerome looked bewildered, then leaned back in his chair and closed his eyes. "I've had to deal with people who thought they weren't getting their fair share," he said, "but I've never before had anyone refuse a bequest. You understand, Mr. Gage, that the property is rightfully and lawfully yours."

"I understand," Frank replied. "I don't think there's any law that says I have to take what I don't want, is there?"

Jerome admitted that there probably was not. He looked from Frank to Augusta. "What do you propose to do about the will?"

Old Mrs. Gage chuckled. "I propose that we chuck it back under the well house and let some future generation worry about it," she suggested. "Augusta, are you going to plant another tree where that one came down?"

"I'd thought about it," Augusta said. "It looks awfully bare out there. Ma was always partial to weeping willows. Might have Hiram set one in for me."

Poor Jerome sighed and lapsed into silence. After the others had visited awhile longer, we rose to leave and Jerome took Len aside. "Do you think they know what they are doing?" he asked anxiously.

"I'm sure they do," Len replied. "Frank Gage is an astute businessman. And Augusta wouldn't be an easy one to fool. Yes, they've settled things to their satisfaction."

"But they haven't settled anything!" Jerome exclaimed. "I'm standing here with a will, a deed, and a transfer. What do we do now?"

"Come, Mr. Grayson," Augusta said soothingly. "I think I have a solution that will benefit all of us. Since Frank doesn't want it, I'll sell two square miles of river land to you for your lumber mill. Then I'll leave the money in my will as a trust for the children. He won't object to that, will you, Frank?"

Frank grinned broadly. "Why, no, Augusta, if that's what you want to do. You don't owe me a thing, you know."

"I'm not paying you anything," Augusta returned. "Just trying to carry out at least part of John's wishes. His children would have inherited it if he and Marcie had lived." She turned to us. "Are we standing here in the doorway all night, or are we going home?"

"Home," Len laughed, and he herded a dazed Jerome out to the buggy.

"That's nearly a thousand acres, Augusta," I said to her after the men had gone on. "That should produce a lot of lumber. What made you change your mind about selling?"

Augusta dropped into the rocker before she answered. "When I learned that none of the property was mine, I realized that there are more important things in life than just holding on to family possessions. A lumber mill will bring jobs and people to this area. Besides, I like that Mr. Grayson. I like the way he does business. I want to see what the Lord can do with a young man like that."

She rose and started for her room. "This has been a long day. You can sit out here if you want to. I'm going to bed."

12

Len Has an Offer

B Y THE SECOND WEEK OF NOVEMBER WE
were deep in preparation for the centennial pageant. We divided the program into four twenty-five year segments,
and the older students were writing the
narrative.

"My grandma started school in 1816, and
George's grandpa started in 1817," Joel Gage
announced. "Does anyone else have folks
that were here in the first quarter?"

There were none, so George and Joel took
charge of that generation. In addition to
school happenings, they were to find any
important things that occurred in the country's history during those years. The other
students divided up the periods left; Edward
was delighted to be assigned 1842-1866.

"Good!" he crowed. "We get the War Between the States! That's the most exciting
thing that's happened in the last hundred
years. I hope there's another war when I'm
old enough to be in it."

"There's a war in our house every day,

120

with you around," Hannah sniffed. "You never wait for the government to declare one."

Edward started to retort.

"Don't start one here," I warned. "We haven't a minute longer than we need to finish this program."

The next morning Joel appeared with a package wrapped in brown paper and tied with string. I could hear the others trying to find out what it contained.

"You'll see when school starts," he told them. "Miss O'Dell has to open it."

"Is it a present for her?" Carrie asked.

"Nope. It won't do you any good to guess, because I won't tell." He put the package on my desk.

"You'll like it. It's for our program," he whispered, then rushed outside to play.

I eyed the bundle, thinking about the surprises I'd already had this year. I hoped this one would have no unpleasant consequences.

The children waited impatiently for opening exercises to be completed. When the pledge to the flag was over and everyone was seated, I picked up the package.

"Are we ready to open it, Joel?" I asked.

He bobbed his head eagerly. "My grandma sent them for our program," he said.

"They're almost as old as she is."

Inside I found two ancient schoolbooks, one a reader and the other a volume of history.

"She used those in school," Joel informed us. "She found them in her trunk. You have to read what they say inside."

I opened the history book and read the poem inscribed on the cover page.

"If flood should hit
And wash you out,
You have no need to cry.
Of all the items in the room
This book will still be dry!"

The children laughed and clapped their hands. "What does the other one say, Miss O'Dell?" they wanted to know. "Does it have a poem, too?"

"Oh, it does! It does!" Joel shouted. "Read it to us, Miss O'Dell."

"When you knock on heaven's gate,
And they open up the same,
When you ask St. Peter there to let you in,
He will shake his head in sorrow
And remind you of your sin
For you've kept a book that
Clearly bears my name!"

"We'll take especially good care of these, Joel," I said when the children were quiet again. "Tell your grandmother how much we appreciate them. If anyone else wants to bring something for display table, it will be a fine addition to the program."

"The children are having a good time collecting all the information," I told Augusta that evening, "and I'm delighted with the extra work they do in math and history and writing. They're learning without even knowing it!"

"Some of them may be surprised by what they learn," Augusta chuckled. "I remember that Paul Alexander, Edward's pa, was pretty fond of Amelia Mathews when he was a youngster."

"So that's where the valentine in the cornerstone came from!" I laughed. "Does Edward's mother know about it?"

"Oh, yes," Augusta replied. "She and Amelia were good friends."

"How many couples do you suppose there are who started out in the North Branch school?" I wondered.

"Don't know," Augusta admitted, "but I can't remember many schoolteachers who married local boys."

"I think it's a nice precedent," I declared, "though I don't suppose everyone in town would agree with me."

"Here comes someone who does," Augusta said, peering out the window. "He looks pretty happy about something."

Len came in on a blast of cold air and took off his mittens and scarf. "Have you ladies had your supper?" he inquired cheerfully. "You're both invited to the Graysons' this evening. Jerome has some plans to talk over with us."

Augusta settled back in her rocker. "You two run along," she said. "My old bones need to stay by the heat tonight."

"Are you feeling all right, Augusta?" I asked anxiously. "Do you want me to stay with you?"

"Mercy sakes!" she sputtered. "Can't a body put her feet up by her own fire without someone thinking she needs a nursemaid?"

"Something is up," I said to Len on the way to Graysons'. "Augusta doesn't turn down the chance to hear firsthand news for any reason."

"She may just feel like staying in," Len said. "You're too suspicious. Anyway, I can ride all the way over there with my arm around you, and I couldn't do that if Augusta came along."

We were soon seated in the Graysons' comfortable living room, and Jerome wasted no time in coming to the reason for our visit.

"I have the plans ready for the lumber

mill," he said, spreading out a map. "Here is the river, and here is the Pere Marquette Railway line. Logs can be sent down the river to the mill here," he pointed to an X on the map, "made into lumber, and shipped out. We'll have to clear enough land to set up a camp here. Do you realize how many men that will employ?"

"That looks wonderful," Len exclaimed. "Will you begin clearing this winter?"

"I hope to," Jerome replied. "It will be spring before the mill can be built and summer before it can operate fully. But we're on the way toward putting North Branch on the map!"

"I can't believe how fast you've made your plans," I said. "You've only known that you could have the land for a little over a week."

Jerome laughed. "I don't leave anything to chance," he said. "I started preparing for that property the moment I saw it; then fate played right into my hand."

Len spoke up. "Nothing happens just by chance. We believe in a God who directs our paths."

"You keep on believing that if it makes you feel better," Jerome replied. "But I didn't ask you out here just to show you a map and tell you about the mill. I have an offer to make, and you and Mabel should hear it

125

together, because it will affect both of you."

"Sounds pretty serious," Len said.

Jerome nodded. "It is. I've come to respect you a great deal in the two months I've been here, Len. I want to ask you to go into partnership with me."

Len looked startled. "But I haven't any money to invest in a business," he protested. "I own a portion of my father's land and haven't enough money to put a house on it. Where would I get funds like that?"

Jerome shook his head. "You don't understand. I don't need money; I need an honest, intelligent man. I'm offering you a half interest in the mill if you'll be my business manager. I'll throw in a section of the land for a house, and by spring you'll have all the money you'll need to build."

There was silence in the room, and over the thumping of my heart I was conscious of the snapping fire and steaming teakettle. Myra was cutting cake, and I rose to help her.

"I never expected anything like this," Len said slowly. "I don't know how to answer."

"I don't need a decision right now," Jerome assured him. "You and Mabel think on it for a few days. You can even pray over it, or whatever it is you do about such things. I'm sure you'll agree, though, that you haven't received a better offer than that today."

Len took a plate of cake from Myra and thanked her absently.

"Let me know before the first of the year," Jerome went on. "By that time I'll have the paperwork done and ready to sign. This business could make us wealthy men, you know."

If Len answered him, I didn't hear it, for my mind was spinning.

As soon as we were in the buggy and on our way home, Len turned to me excitedly. "Mabel, just think—we could have a beautiful home and anything you want. It sure sounds like an answer to prayer. And you'd never have to work again!"

Haven't we been through all this before? I thought, but Len sounded so happy, I didn't say a word. I was glad it was too dark to see my face. I bit my lip to keep from blurting out what I was thinking, and Len in his euphoria didn't notice my silence.

Augusta was waiting for us when we arrived, and Len told her the amazing news.

"Can you believe it!" she responded. "It sounds as though you're planning to say yes."

"Well," Len replied, "it certainly looks like an opportunity from the Lord. There is no end to the miracles the storm produced."

He retrieved his hat and mittens from the chair. "I'll let you ladies retire. See you before you leave tomorrow, Mabel."

He ran out to the buggy. I closed the door slowly behind him, then leaned against it.

Augusta was watching me carefully. "You don't look overjoyed about this great miracle, Mabel. Doesn't the idea of a big, new home sound good to you?"

"What about the ministry, Augusta? What about Len's call from the Lord? Is God really taking that back and sending the lumber mill in its place?"

"Did you ask Len those questions?"

"No. This is his decision. I don't want to influence him."

"I don't claim to be an authority on marriage," Augusta declared, "but if anyone should be allowed to influence a man, it's his wife. And that's what you're planning to be."

I went to bed and thought for a long time not just about Augusta's words but about something Jerome had said a week earlier: "People tend to temper their ideals when large amounts of money are involved."

I prayed that Jerome would be wrong this time, too.

13
Ma Sends Her Love

"SARAH JANE, WHEN TIME IS DIVIDED SO neatly into months and weeks, wouldn't you think life's trials and tribulations could be distributed more evenly?" We were on our way home for the weekend, happy for some time to catch up with each other.

"How do you want them spaced?" she asked. "Three trials a week and four tribulations monthly? What happened to 'Casting all your care upon him, for he careth for you'?"

"Do you realize you've been quoting Scripture to me since we learned our first verses in Sunday school fifteen years ago?"

"That's because I like short, well-phrased words of wisdom. They also happen to be true. You're evading the question."

"I know," I sighed. "There's not one thing I can do about either of the two matters that concern me most. The Lord is going to take care of Ma without any help from me. Your mother has promised to be there as soon as she is called, and Pa can get the doctor in less than half an hour. I know they don't need me."

"You're right about that," Sarah Jane agreed. "You'd be worse than useless pacing around the kitchen, wringing your hands. But I'm not so sure about the other concern."

"Jerome didn't offer *me* the job," I protested. "It has to be Len's decision."

"But it's your life, too, Mabel. It's just that you and I have a different approach to problem solving. You fuss to yourself and never face anyone with what you really think."

I nodded. "I know. You would have reminded Len of his responsibility to the Lord before he'd had a chance to think about how rich he could be. I guess I figured that was the Lord's job."

"You're right, too," Sarah Jane said. "You can't make up Len's mind for him, and he shouldn't feel obligated to do what you think is best." She shrugged. "I'm just a run-the-world person."

"That's the way I like you," I assured her. "And so does Thomas. By the way, what do you hear from him? When will he be home?"

"For Thanksgiving," she replied. "He works Saturdays as a lab assistant in the science department. It's a good job, and he can keep it full-time this summer if he wants." Sarah Jane glanced at me. "He wants us to get married before school starts next fall."

"Married! But he has another year of school! And what about your job at Edenville?"

"I'm not as dedicated to teaching as you are, Mabel," she said with a grin. "I'd rather be Mrs. Thomas Charles. Besides, Thomas says I won't have a problem getting a position in Ann Arbor if I want to teach."

"You've decided, then."

"Well, of course, I'm asking your permission first," Sarah Jane teased.

"Our lives will really be going separate ways, won't they?" I said. "I don't know how to handle that, Sarah Jane. We've never been more than a few miles apart as long as we've lived."

Sarah Jane nodded. "I've thought about that a lot. But nothing can take away the years of our lives that we've shared—we'll remember them when we're old ladies."

"You're right, as usual," I said.

"Besides," Sarah Jane reminded me, "You've as much as told me I couldn't live with you after you were married, anyway! You'll have to manufacture your own problems from now on."

"That shouldn't be hard," I laughed. "But I'm glad the Lord arranged for me to meet Len."

"Are you sure it was the Lord?" Sarah Jane snickered. "It looked an awful lot like a goat to me!"

"You are never going to forget that, are you?" I said with a sigh.

"Not the longest day I live. The sight of that animal chasing you into Len's arms—when you didn't even know who Len was—is among my choicest memories." Then she grew more sober. "But I agree—the Lord directs the decisions of our lives if we allow Him to. Haven't you ever wondered whom you might have met if you had taken a different school?"

I shook my head. "Len is the one I want. He's sensible and patient and levelheaded enough for both of us. And he'll need to be," I added hastily before Sarah Jane could say it.

"In addition to all that, he thinks you're the best thing that has happened to North Branch since the railroad went through," she said. "You couldn't ask for much more."

I left Sarah Jane at her porch with a promise to see her later and turned toward home. Pa met me and took my things from the buggy.

"Ma's lying down," he told me as he

prepared to lead Regal to the barn.

"Is anything wrong?" I asked in alarm.

"No, no," Pa assured me. "She's fine. A mite uncomfortable is all." He chuckled. "She's sure it didn't take this long the last time."

I hurried into the house to find Ma coming down the hallway toward the kitchen.

"I thought I heard voices," she said cheerfully. "I'm glad you're home."

"Go back and lie down, Ma. I'll come in there and talk to you."

"I don't want to lie down," she said, "but come back here and let me show you what the ladies at the church brought this week."

We went to her room, and Ma took out a box of handmade baby things. "Aren't they beautiful? This will be the best dressed baby I ever had. Pa brought the old cradle down from the attic and refinished it. This is all beginning to seem more real to me now."

"What will you call the baby, Ma?"

"That depends first of all—"

"It's a girl," I stated.

Ma laughed. "If it's a girl, you may name her."

"I can't believe I was ever small enough to fit in there," I said, looking at the cradle.

"You're not much bigger than that now," Ma replied, eyeing me critically. "Have you been losing some weight?"

"I don't see how I could be, with Augusta fixing the meals," I said. "She's always after me to eat more."

I didn't tell Ma about my concern over Len's decision, figuring she didn't need anything to upset her right now. *That's just a part of growing up,* I thought. *You have to fight your own battles.*

I shared my thoughts with Sarah Jane as we traveled back on Sunday.

"Parents do all they can to smooth the road for you, but in the end you have to make your own way, don't you? I didn't say a word to Pa and Ma about Jerome's offer."

"If you keep that up, you'll find out you really can run your own life," Sarah Jane replied. "And don't forget that your folks had some expert help in bringing you up."

"You?"

"That, too, of course," she grinned. "But I was thinking how fortunate we've been to have parents who trusted the Lord for guidance. I hope I do as well with my children."

Len was still excited about the prospect of a partnership with Jerome. After church that evening he talked about our home.

"Would you rather be near the river or closer in to town? Let's ride around this week and choose a likely spot. Do you want a one-story house that's spread out or two stories? Maybe we should look at some places in town to get some ideas." He sighed happily. "Isn't God good to give us all this?"

Len didn't seem to notice that I wasn't as joyful about the whole affair as he was. Perhaps I was wrong. Maybe the Lord *did* send this good fortune our way. It was certainly no sin to take advantage of the best life had to offer, was it? Then why did I feel so miserable about the whole thing?

"What did your folks say about it?" I asked.

Len didn't answer for a moment. "I haven't told them," he said. "I thought I'd wait until we have the arrangements all worked out. They'll probably be disappointed, but I'm sure they'll see what a wonderful opportunity this is. After all, there's no reason I can't continue to work for the Lord. In fact, I'll probably have more contacts at the mill than I ever would in a tiny little church."

The last of November was here, and we had just two weeks left to get ready for our program. Jamie was concerned about the decorating.

"We've never had a Christmas without our own tree," he announced. "Just because this isn't exactly a *Christmas* pageant doesn't mean we should skip all that."

"We always have time for the Christmas story, no matter what else we do," I agreed. "We must have a tree and a manger! The other decorations will have to do with the school's history."

When I arrived home on Wednesday afternoon, Augusta met me at the door. "You took long enough to get here."

"I came as soon as the children left," I told her. "Did you need something?"

"No, I don't need a thing. Just wanted to tell you that your pa has a real odd sense of humor."

"Pa! Is he here?"

"Nope. He sent you that card over there."

I dropped my books on the chair and ran to get the postcard.

> *The baby came this morning. Everyone is fine. Ma sends her love.*
> *Yours,*
> *Pa*

I read it through twice. "But what *is* it?" I wailed. "Why didn't he say whether it was a boy or a girl? I won't know until Friday!" I looked helplessly at Augusta, and she burst out laughing.

"Be thankful you know it's here, and that your ma is all right," she said. "Some men wouldn't have gotten that much on a card."

"Pa did that on purpose," I said in disgust. "I was so sure I knew what the baby would be that he wants me to stew for a few days."

I looked at the clueless card again and smiled. There was time later on to be annoyed with Pa—right now I was thankful that all was well at home.

"You'll want to go over and tell Len and his folks," Augusta's voice broke in. "Here's a fresh pie for their supper. We have one to celebrate with, too, so hurry back."

I thanked Augusta, put my hat and mittens back on, and stepped outside into a soft snow, one that promised to make the world look as new as the baby at our house.

14

Len's Choice

O N Friday afternoon, Len went to Edenville to get Sarah Jane while I got ready to go home. This was such a special occasion that all three of us were anxious to be on the way. Len would have to be home for Sunday, but Mr. Clark would bring Sarah Jane and me back to school.

Today we didn't let Regal waste any time ambling along the road; we covered the distance as quickly as possible.

"You can't let me off at my place," Sarah Jane said as we neared her lane. "I won't live another ten minutes if I don't know what that baby is. I hate calling it an 'it.' "

"Pa will pay for this," I said.

As soon as the buggy stopped, I jumped down and ran into the house, with Len and Sarah Jane right behind me. Ma was sitting up in bed, smiling happily, and I rushed over to hug her.

"Are you all right, Ma? Is the baby all right?"

"We're both fine," she laughed. "Haven't

you thought of a name for her yet?"

"Then it *is* a girl?"

"Why, of course. Didn't Pa tell you that?" Ma looked perplexed.

I whirled around to see Pa standing in the doorway, grinning broadly.

"Why, no," he said innocently. "I didn't think I had to. Mabel said she knew that it would be a girl."

"Why, Jim, what a thing to do!" Ma chided.

I threw my arms around his neck. "You don't know how I have suffered the last two days."

"When are you going to come and look at her?" Sarah Jane said. "It's been my experience that four-day-old babies have faces you could kiss only if you were related to them, but this one is different. She's actually pretty."

It was true. As I bent over the cradle I thought I had never seen a more beautiful baby. A soft, dark fuzz covered her head, and her eyelashes curled against round, smooth cheeks.

"Are her eyes blue, Ma?"

"They are at the moment," Ma replied. "Dark blue. They may change later. So what are we going to call her?"

"Violet," I replied. "She looks like a little flower."

"That's a pretty name," Ma agreed. "Do you like that, Pa?"

"Yes," Pa said with a nod, "but I can tell you right now that she'll never be a *shrinking* Violet. Wait till you hear her yell. Has a mind of her own already."

"If it's all right with you, I'll retreat home before she gives a demonstration," Sarah Jane laughed. "She's a wonderful baby, Mrs. O'Dell. She'll keep you young for a long time."

"I'll take Sarah Jane home and be right back to help you with the chores," Len said.

"And I'll get supper tonight," I told Pa, "although you don't deserve it."

After they had left, I sat down to talk with Ma. "Have the boys been here?" I asked.

"Oh, yes. I think they're both glad they aren't home any longer. Roy still remembers what a trial you were!"

"I hope he has five daughters," I said cheerfully. "It would take at least that many to make his life as miserable as he made mine!"

The weekend passed quickly, and I could see that Ma wasn't going to lack for plenty to do in the months ahead. Although we hadn't discussed it beforehand, neither Len nor I mentioned his possible change of profession to Pa or Ma. I think we both knew in our hearts that they would be disappointed.

"If the things you worry about the most never happen, I'm going to throw my whole heart into this one," I told Sarah Jane on Sunday. "Jerome wants an answer before Christmas. But actually I'm trying not to worry. I've committed it to the Lord, and I'll accept the result."

"That's a good idea," Sarah Jane agreed, "but I think Len needs to know how you feel, too. He should at least understand that you wouldn't mind being a preacher's wife if that's what the Lord wants."

"I'm sure he knows that. I've certainly tried to show him that I think the ministry is important."

The next two weeks were pandemonium. Regular classes were all but abandoned as the children learned their parts and put the pageant together. I had little opportunity to reflect on the fact that Len was unusually quiet and subdued till his mother mentioned it to me.

"I hope Len isn't worrying about something," she said. "He's so preoccupied that I have to speak to him twice to get an answer. Does he have something on his mind that you know of?"

"He hasn't talked anything over with me,"

I replied truthfully. "The program is taking a lot of his spare time. I'm sure things will get back to normal when that's over." I needed to believe that for my sake as well as hers.

The schoolhouse was packed on the evening of the program. Some who hadn't been near the school in years arrived, eager to renew memories of the past. The children did a beautiful job of portraying their ancestors and bringing a century of history alive. Old Mrs. Gage and Grandpa Elliot were honored as the oldest former students and, as a special surprise, Mr. Rosswell, who had rebuilt the school seventeen years before, appeared and officially appointed a delighted Toby Elliot to be in charge of opening the cornerstone in 1975.

When the last excited child and family had disappeared into the night, I sat down wearily at my desk.

"I think I'll come in tomorrow to clean up," I said to Len. "I just don't have the energy tonight. Do you suppose you could bank the fire so it won't take long to get warm in the morning?"

He nodded and turned to the stove, and I looked around the empty room. Our program had been a huge success.

"Len," I said, "during the Christmas holiday, we need to set the date for our wedding. I know we don't have a house yet, but we could stay with your folks while we get it ready, couldn't we?"

Len had his back to me, and he didn't reply for a long moment. When he did, I was sure that I hadn't heard correctly.

"Mabel, I can't go through with it."

"You . . . you what?"

"I've known for a long time, but I haven't had the heart to tell you." He turned to look at me miserably. "Can you forgive me?"

I thought my breath would never start again. When it did, I said weakly, "Are you . . . going to marry someone else?"

Alarm spread across his face. "Marry someone . . . Are you crazy? I'd never marry anyone but you!" Then it dawned on him, and he strode across the room and took me in his arms. "Oh, Mabel! How could you even *imagine* such a thing! I didn't mean I couldn't marry you!"

I began to sob with relief, and Len patted me awkwardly on the back. "Then what can't you do?" I gulped.

"Jerome's offer," he answered. "I can't accept Jerome's offer. I know you've been planning on a big house and all, but I couldn't live with myself if I rejected God's call for all the wealth of this world. I shouldn't even have considered it."

I slumped back into my chair. "Oh, Len," I said, "I never wanted all those things. I wanted you to stay in the church."

"You did? But why didn't you say so?"

"You seemed so happy and excited that I couldn't," I replied. "If you really wanted the partnership, I didn't want to stand in the way."

"I thought I could make up to you what you were losing by not marrying Russ Bradley," Len said.

"Russ Bradley!" I exclaimed. "Oh, Len. It's you I chose—I don't care if we have to live in a tent."

"I hope that won't be necessary, Mabel. But I know we'll be happy if the Lord is pleased with our lives."

"This will be the best Christmas I've ever had," I told him. "I feel as though a load has been lifted from my shoulders."

Len regarded me soberly. "I hope we've learned a lesson," he said. "I'll never assume that I know what you're thinking again."

"When will you let Jerome know?" I asked.

"Let's go see him tomorrow," Len decided. "I hate to let him down, but it's a matter of conscience. I can't compromise."

Our visit to the Graysons' was an interesting one. Jerome had the plans for the new lumber mill spread out on a table in his office, and he eagerly pointed out the location of all the buildings and equipment. "We're ready to begin," he said. "I've engaged a contractor, and he's started to hire his help. This will be a going concern before you know it. Have you two chosen the section for your house? We'll clear that first."

Len sat down at the table and ran his hand over the plans. "They look wonderful," he said. "This company will be a real boost to the community. Jerome, I appreciate your offer to make me a partner, more than I can say. But I'm afraid I have to decline. I'm sorry, but—I already have a task I'm called to do."

Jerome looked startled, then he studied Len quietly. After a moment, he turned and looked out the window. "Perhaps I shouldn't admit this," Jerome said finally, "but I suspected that's what you would say. I've watched your life and your commitment to what I thought was a foolish endeavor. I've always believed people were out to get all they could, however they could. But you were so sure that Miss Harris and Frank Gage weren't like that—and events proved you correct." Jerome went over and sat down behind his desk. "You're the kind of man I'd like to be in business with, Len," he continued, "but I think I would have been disappointed if you had said yes. You really believe what you say about the Christian life. And I'd like to believe, too."

Len was quiet on the way home. "To think that greed could have cost me the opportunity to lead someone to the Lord," he said. "God can use Jerome in the lumber mill, but that isn't where God wants me. How close I came to making a wrong choice!" He squeezed my hand and smiled at me. "I didn't make a wrong choice when I lifted *you* out of the path of that goat, did I?"

"No, you didn't," I replied. "But I'd be just as happy if you and Sarah Jane would not choose to remind me of it quite so often!"

15

Adding New Dimensions

"MA SAYS YOU HAVE TO WINTER AND summer a man before you really know him." Sarah Jane shared this information with Augusta and me as we sat together sewing one morning in early spring.

"So I've heard," Augusta replied. "You find out his true character when he hits a rough spot in the road. Have you wintered Thomas yet?"

"Probably not as seriously as I will in the future!" she laughed. "But I know one important thing about him—he can laugh at himself."

"That's essential to survive around you," I said. "If I hadn't learned that, I'd have spent half my life in tears."

"You must admit that you've done a few funny things, Mabel—some of which we won't mention." Her eyes danced as she looked at me.

"Tell Augusta what Thomas did last winter," I said quickly. "That was proof that you're getting a good-natured husband."

"Thomas was visiting last January," Sarah Jane related, "and he offered to help Pa with the chores. It was so cold the snow squeaked. When Thomas couldn't put his hands on something to break the ice in the trough, he decided to jump on it. That worked fine, but he went in over his boot tops. He was embarrassed to tell Pa what a stupid thing he had done, so he went right on in to milk instead of taking off those wet socks. By the time they came to the house, his socks and shoes and boots were frozen solid. He stood by the door till Ma noticed him and told him to sit down and take his boots off. Then he had to confess." Sarah Jane chuckled. "I told myself I would *not* laugh at him, he looked so chagrined, but by the time we had him thawed out, he was laughing so hard I had to pull the boots off for him!"

"You can weather a lot of storms with good humor," Augusta agreed. "Have you and Thomas settled on a date for your wedding?"

"The end of the summer," Sarah Jane replied. "Our rooms at the university aren't ready until the term begins. I'm not fortunate enough to move into a house like you are, Mabel. How is it coming, anyway?"

"Just fine," I said happily. "Len says it will be ready for us to begin work on the inside as soon as we are married."

Sarah Jane shook her head. "I'd never be able to stand it. I'd want to inspect every nail, but you haven't even gone to look at it!"

"I promised. Len wants to have it all ready to decorate before I see it, then we'll do that part together. I told him I'd like anything as long as I could see the river and had a road to get in and out on.

"One reason I chose an April date was so we could be settled before school starts next fall. Ma thinks it will be hard to finish the school year and fix up a house at the same time, but we can do it." I snipped off a thread on the hem I was sewing. "Besides, Len wants to begin cultivating as soon as it thaws, and I want to get my garden in. June is too late for that."

"What do the children think about it?" Sarah Jane wanted to know. "Remember how thrilled we were over Miss Gibson's wedding?"

"The children are excited. George's father promised to bring all of them over in the hay wagon. There will be more people from North Branch than from my own home town!"

"Gracious! Where will you put them all?" Augusta said.

"We'll be married in the yard," I said.

"Right out under the trees. All the impor- tant parties I've ever had were in that yard. There's no other place for it."

"And if it rains?" Sarah Jane suggested.

"It wouldn't *dare!*"

And it didn't. As I leaned out my window that perfect April morning, the scent of early lilacs wafted up to me and a breeze stirred my hair. I could hear Ma in the kitchen talk- ing to the baby. I had seen Pa go to the barn, and I knew that before very long I would have to plunge into this day and be carried along, ready or not.

My thoughts turned to Len, with his dark, wavy hair and laughing eyes. I thanked the Lord for sending him my way, and smiled to myself as I imagined Sarah Jane saying, "Are you sure it was the Lord? . . . " I knew that it was, and if God were willing, Len and I would spend many happy years together.

I looked around my room. My trunk was packed, ready to go with us to our new home. My other belongings had been moved a bit at a time by Len and his father.

My wedding dress, lovingly made by Augusta, lay across the bed. "It's nice enough to be married in and will be serviceable for a long time," she had informed me. "You have to be practical when you're a preacher's wife." I fingered the soft, gray material and thought how fond I'd become of Augusta. How different people appear to you when you've "summered and wintered" them. I would miss her sharp tongue and loving wisdom.

"Mabel! It's almost eight o'clock and you're sitting there dreaming!"

I jumped guiltily at the sound of Sarah Jane's voice. She plunked herself on the bed and looked around the room.

"I understand. Milestone markers take some thinking on. But if we're going to have things ready before the guests arrive, you'll have to think on your feet." She jumped up and pulled me with her, then hugged me tight.

"You've been the best friend anyone ever had," she said. "An awful lot of responsibility, but worth it."

Len and I had decided on a morning service so that there would be time for a leisurely reception before the guests needed to start home for evening chores. We had also discussed the possibility of rain.

"We can open the doors between the parlor and the rest of the rooms," Ma had said. "It won't look as spacious as the yard, but we can bring in the lilacs and daffodils and greenery to decorate the parlor."

But second best wasn't necessary. When Pa and I were ready to walk the short distance between the house and the arbor set up in the yard, the sun was shining brightly and the sky was a heavenly blue.

"I like that Mr. Grayson," Pa said, as Jerome took his place with Len beside the minister. "I'm glad you and Len will have such good friends in the community."

Sarah Jane walked ahead of us, and her pale green dress blended nicely with the arbutus and wispy fern that she carried. I carried a bouquet of my favorite spring flowers—narcissus, lily of the valley, and orchid lilacs nestled in maidenhair fern.

Pa squeezed my arm gently as he left me at Len's side and went to stand by Ma. Violet watched with wide blue eyes, and I was glad I had convinced Ma to bring the baby out for the ceremony.

Our minister, Reverend Barrett, smiled happily as he began the service. "Dearly beloved, we are gathered here in the presence of God and these witnesses. . . ."

"These witnesses" were my dear family and friends. Surely no one was more blessed than I to have all these people around me on my special day. Mollie and Warren were there, as well as Jacob and Lettie and other friends from high school days. Russ and

Clarice did not come, though I would have been happy to see them. Amelia Mathews baked the wedding cake, and she and Myra Grayson were hostesses for the reception. Elsie, Prudence, Carrie and Serena proudly served the guests. My whole wedding day was a beautiful expression of friendship.

It was early evening before Len and I started back to North Branch. "My, it's quiet," I said. "I haven't heard this much silence for weeks."

"I know," Len agreed. "Wasn't it great to have so many wonderful friends at our wedding? And it was nice of your folks to have Ma and Pa stay over till tomorrow. Would you rather stay at their place tonight and see our house tomorrow morning?"

"No, I want to begin our life together in our own home," I replied. "Is everything there that we need to start housekeeping?"

Len nodded happily. "I had advice from both Ma and Augusta. You know they wouldn't forget anything."

'Have they been to see it?"

"No, I wanted you to be the first. Besides, we have a lot of fixing up to do before we have company. I brought in only the basic necessities."

Aside from the fact that I knew there were

three small rooms, I had no idea what the house would look like. I knew I could change anything except the structure, but I braced myself for surprises.

"We'll have to stop and take care of Pa's chores." Len's voice broke into my thoughts. "Do you think we should take some milk and eggs for breakfast in the morning?"

"Isn't there any food there?"

"Well, no. I've been too busy to think about food. Maybe we could eat with the folks for a few days."

For a moment I didn't know what to say. What a way to begin our married life! "That's all right. I'll find enough for us to eat tomorrow, and we'll go into town for supplies. You did take dishes and linens over, didn't you?"

"Oh, yes. I took over everything you had packed. I can't wait for you to see it, Mabel."

I could wait, I decided, as I gathered food from the Williamses' pantry and tried to imagine what else Len might not have thought to provide. But he was so pleased about everything that I made up my mind to act delighted, no matter what was missing.

It was dark by the time he had finished feeding and milking.

"We'll be there in ten minutes," Len said happily as he tucked the food basket into the buggy. As we rounded the grove of trees on our lot, I heard the river rushing by and saw the dim outline of the small house. Len stopped Regal in the front and jumped down from the buggy.

"Here we are," he said. "Welcome to your new home, Mabel." He lifted me out and set me down. Then he took a step toward the house and threw open the door. The light of the moon through the trees was very dim. I leaned against the doorpost.

"Can you light the lantern, Len?"

Silence. "I don't believe there's one here," he said finally.

"No light?"

"I've just been working during the day, and I haven't needed it," he explained apologetically. "But let's unload the buggy and I'll go back to the house and get one. It won't take more than twenty minutes."

Together we transferred the trunk and the food to the floor of the main room.

"Do you want to go with me?"

"I'll wait here," I replied. "I like the smell of the new wood."

He turned the buggy around, and as he disappeared from sight I sank down on my trunk and laughed until I cried. As Sarah Jane would have said, it was a most unpropitious beginning.

I sat looking out the window at the trees—our trees—waiting for Len to return. It occurred to me that as milestones go, this one promised to point toward a future every bit as unpredictable as the past. And I knew that there was no one I would rather spend that future with than Len.

Away from Home

When you're sixteen, everything is momentous.

That's what Mabel's best friend Sarah Jane tells her as they begin their first year of school at the academy in town. Away from their farm homes and families for the first time, the two girls must contend with a new school, new acquaintances, and new ways of doing things.

And Sarah Jane is right. Whether it's wearing bloomers for physical culture class, mustering the courage to invite young men to an evening social event, or helping the housekeeper with a routine task, the two friends have a way of making "momentous moments" out of anything. Mabel and Sarah Jane rise to each occasion with their usual measure of hilarity, anguish, and new-found insights, all the while learning more of what it means to place one's trust in God.

The Grandma's Attic Novels bring you the story of Mabel O'Dell's young adult years as she becomes a teacher, wife, and mother. Be sure to read all five!

Away from Home
A School of Her Own
Wedding Bells Ahead
At Home in North Branch
New Faces, New Friends

Gifted storyteller **Arleta Richardson** grew up an only child in Chicago, living in a hotel on the shores of Lake Michigan. Under the care of her maternal grandmother, she listened for hours as her grandmother told stories from her own childhood. With unusual recall, Arleta began to write these stories for an audience that now numbers over 2 million. "My grandmother would be amazed to know her stories have gone around the world," Arleta says.

Cook Communications

A School of Her Own

"Are we *really* ready to be schoolteachers?"

There are times when Mabel isn't too sure, despite the optimistic encouragement of her best friend, Sarah Jane. Cold stoves, scarlet fever, and a break-in at the schoolhouse are only part of her worries in her first year of teaching. How should she handle the threats of Cy Lawton, whose son comes to school bearing the marks of his father's anger? Or the gossip about her "setting her cap" for Leonard Williams, the young minister?

Meanwhile, letters from her high school friend Russ keep coming, regular as clockwork, offering Mabel a comfortable, secure future as a banker's wife. Mabel thinks she is too young to be facing such important decisions even with God's help, but as Sarah Jane reminds her, "Life keeps moving on, whether you're ready or not."

The Grandma's Attic Novels bring you the story of Mabel O'Dell's young adult years as she becomes a teacher, wife, and mother. Be sure to read all five!

Away from Home
A School of Her Own
Wedding Bells Ahead
At Home in North Branch
New Faces, New Friends

Gifted storyteller **Arleta Richardson** grew up an only child in Chicago, living in a hotel on the shores of Lake Michigan. Under the care of her maternal grandmother, she listened for hours as her grandmother told stories from her own childhood. With unusual recall, Arleta began to write these stories for an audience that now numbers over 2 million. "My grandmother would be amazed to know her stories have gone around the world," Arleta says.

Cook Communications

At Home in North Branch

At home in North Branch—what could be better?

Happy with Len in their little house by the river, surrounded by friends, Mabel is content with her life as a schoolteacher and minister's wife in the small logging community. But a storm is about to break over North Branch, and no one in town will be left untouched.

Meet Rowland Brewer, the new manager of the shingle mill: handsome, friendly . . . and just a shade too smooth. Meet his daughter, Daisy: the sweetest, prettiest ten year old ever seen . . . at least at first glance.

And get reacquainted with the Lawton clan, still holding a grudge against Mabel . . . Augusta Harris, still keeping track of everyone's comings and goings . . . and of course Sarah Jane, who has moved back into Mabel's life to remind her that the Lord will help her weather every trial.

The Grandma's Attic Novels bring you the story of Mabel O'Dell's young adult years as she becomes a teacher, wife, and mother. Be sure to read all five!

Away from Home
A School of Her Own
Wedding Bells Ahead
At Home in North Branch
New Faces, New Friends

Gifted storyteller **Arleta Richardson** grew up an only child in Chicago, living in a hotel on the shores of Lake Michigan. Under the care of her maternal grandmother, she listened for hours as her grandmother told stories from her own childhood. With unusual recall, Arleta began to write these stories for an audience that now numbers over 2 million. "My grandmother would be amazed to know her stories have gone around the world," Arleta says.

Cook Communications

New Faces, New Friends

Who says a small town is a dull place to live?

The logging community of North Branch, Michigan, is still a small town in 1895. But Mabel and Len Williams and their circle of friends could never be called bored. . . .

Mabel finds that her position as the minister's wife doesn't protect her from small town gossip. After all, isn't it a little odd that Hudson Curtis, pastor of a neighboring church, happens to show up every time Mabel comes to town? And wasn't that his buggy seen turning down Mabel's lane the other afternoon? Even Mabel's best friend, Sarah Jane, seems troubled about something—but for the first time in her life, she won't discuss it with Mabel.

Good thing Mabel knows she can trust God in the troubled times as well as the good.

The Grandma's Attic Novels bring you the story of Mabel O'Dell's young adult years as she becomes a teacher, wife, and mother. Be sure to read all five!

Away from Home
A School of Her Own
Wedding Bells Ahead
At Home in North Branch
New Faces, New Friends

Gifted storyteller **Arleta Richardson** grew up an only child in Chicago, living in a hotel on the shores of Lake Michigan. Under the care of her maternal grandmother, she listened for hours as her grandmother told stories from her own childhood. With unusual recall, Arleta began to write these stories for an audience that now numbers over 2 million. "My grandmother would be amazed to know her stories have gone around the world," Arleta says.

Cook Communications